FALLEN KING

COURT OF THE SEA FAE — BOOK TWO

C.N. CRAWFORD

1

AENOR

From a window in the fortress, I gazed down at the streets of Acre. Dusk stained the sky blood red. I was nearly out of time here at the Court of the Sea Fae.

Salem was coming for me. He'd told me himself in the messages he'd been sending.

On the horizon, a few clouds were rolling in, sliding over the ruddy sky. Tonight, I'd been left to stew in my own worries. The other knights had left to fight an impending vampire threat, and silence hung over the ancient castle.

But despite the quiet, my pulse was racing. My time here was nearly up, and tension coiled my body. If I looked out to the right, I had a view of the seawall, and the churning sea crashing against it. If I were a powerful sorcerer like the Merrow, I could bring down the sea on Salem...

A flicker of movement caught my eye, and my pulse kicked up a notch. I stared at the raven fluttering toward my window. Another message from Salem. I already knew what the paper it carried would say.

Even so, as the raven opened its beak and dropped the scrap onto the windowsill, my heart skipped a beat.

I picked it up and unfurled it, my mouth going dry. It simply read: *I'm coming for you soon*—signed by Salem in an elegant, looping script.

This was the second note Salem had sent me. A message straight from hell. Long fingers of dread crept over my heart like afternoon shadows.

Salem didn't tell me *when* he was coming, or what he wanted with me. He just wanted the fear to grow in my chest like a seed, the roots of panic to twine around my ribs. He was, to his credit, doing a decent job of freaking me out.

I gripped the windowsill, staring out at Acre. Looking for him.

Fine. Come and get me, you monster. Because I'm going to find a way to kill you for good.

With my jaw set tight, I shoved Salem's note into my pocket, scanning the streets below. Would he send henchmen for me, or would he come on his own? Maybe I wouldn't see a single sign before he rolled in. I'd just hear the dreadful sound of his rhythmic, booming magic, and it would all be over.

Damn. If he wanted to screw with my head, he was doing a fine job. I pulled a packet of gum out of my skirt pocket and popped a piece in my mouth. Wintergreen usually calmed my nerves.

I took a deep breath, focusing on the mint and the sea breeze. Right now, the silence in the castle hung heavy.

I hummed to myself—"*Suspicious Minds.*" Elvis would keep me sane. I needed noise. Music. Distractions. I leaned down on the windowsill, gazing out at the ancient city, and sang to myself.

As I stared at the city streets, I was startled to see a lick of fiery magic piercing the twilight.

Salem? He was the fiery type.

Flames seemed to follow him wherever he went, and he smelled of smoke. And then there were his eyes... His eyes looked like a twilight sky over a burning city. So what was this moving flame in the city?

My muscles tensed, and I strained my eyes to get a better look. On the raised street that curved along the oceanside, a magical creature stalked. Ghostly flames snaked from his body. Just like I'd seen with Salem.

But apart from that, the creature didn't look a thing like my worst enemy. While Salem was beautiful and elegant, this thing had a gnarled body and loping gait. Like an animal. A demon, maybe? I had to get a closer look.

It took me a few minutes to realize he was following someone—a woman wearing headphones. She didn't seem to notice the monster behind her. As he walked, the trees lining the street seemed to decay, leaves browning and withering to black. The scent of smoke tinged the air, his fingertips blazing.

Hells. Was this one of Salem's henchmen?

But he didn't seem like he was coming for me. Instead, he seemed intent on the woman ahead of him, closing the gap between them. I waited for one of the humans by the seawall to warn her. Oddly, none of them seemed to notice.

I glanced at the horizon, where storm clouds had gathered in the darkening sky. Thunder rumbled. In the next few moments, heavy rain started to fall.

When I glanced back at the fiery creature, I saw that rain had doused some of the flames over his fingertips. Curls of dark smoke coiled into the air from his body. But within moments, the flames were back, his fingertips burning like flesh candles.

"Hey!" I cupped my hands to shout at the woman. "There's a demon behind you! *Demon!*"

My voice floated helplessly away on the sea breeze. It was lost in the sound of the crashing waves and the traffic.

Gods damn it.

My jaw tightened. I supposed the demon wasn't going to kill itself, was it?

I didn't particularly want to leave the fortress walls, but I wasn't going to stand here doing nothing while a woman burned to death. I snatched a cloak off the bed—moss green —and draped it over my shoulders.

Then I grabbed a sword and a sheath, slinging them around my waist. It had been a long time since I'd used a sword, but I'd been trained once.

Now armed, I rushed through the hall, hoping I could get to the woman before anything terrible happened.

And if I was *very* good at my task, maybe I could even get the creature to tell me what he was.

On the lowest level, it took a few minutes for the fortress's heavy gate to open, then I rushed out into the courtyard. With the storm overhead, shadows absorbed the walls around me.

The sound of a woman's screaming told me I needed to run faster, and I broke into a sprint, rushing through the castle's outer gate. Rain dampened my cloak, wetting my cheeks.

But—bizarrely—as I ran, the air started to heat. Around me, it was growing warmer, drier. Now, it was almost like the rain was evaporating in the air around me.

If it was raining, why did it feel dry as a bone out here?

Suddenly, the rainstorm had turned into desert air, the

heat scratching my throat. When I rounded the corner toward the seawall, I caught sight of the woman. My pulse raced out of control.

Something had scalded her skin. Red magic beamed around her, warming the air. My throat was parched, rough as sand. *So dry...*

Heat blazed beneath my feet, like I was standing on the surface of the sun. For a second, I just stared, trying to figure out what I was seeing.

Then the creature swiped for the woman. When his flaming fingertips struck her sweatshirt, her clothes ignited.

Okay. Time to act.

I ran toward the woman and pulled off my cloak, wrapping it around her to douse the flames.

I whirled to find the demon staring at me, and I unsheathed my sword. Within seconds, the tip of my blade was at his throat. He stared at me like he wasn't scared. Like he'd already seen something worse than death.

My stomach tightened. This *thing* was drying, burning the air. Turning everything to dust, sucking up the very rain around us.

And this close, I could see he wasn't a demon. He was a bestial fae, old as the rocks. Muscles gnarled his body like an old oak. When he smiled at me, he exposed a row of rotten teeth, and his eyes flickered with pale flames. He had the earthy, mossy scent of a fae, and the delicately pointed ears, too.

What was he? He was nothing I'd ever seen before. Old and warped.

Heat radiated from his body, singeing the air and parching my mouth. I tried to swallow, but it felt like glass in my throat.

I pressed the blade closer, ready to take off his head.

But first, I wanted some answers. "Did Salem send you?"

"Salem..." he rasped, his grin broadening. "Salem... the evening star... the fallen king of Mag Mell..."

"Ah. You're acquainted."

"He will set us free..."

I knew it. "Do you work for him?"

"We... are..." He spoke in a choked tone, eyes wide. The sound of his voice sent chills up my neck. "We are... the oldest ones. We are... the buried ones. You made us... suffer. We will punish..."

He reached for me, and red, heated air blazed from his fingertips like claws. Then his face contorted with rage.

I swung for him, the blade carving through his neck. It only took a moment, and his head rolled across the pavement, flames snuffing out.

I stared as his corpse shimmered away like a desert mirage. Then—all at once—the air cooled, and the rain started falling again. It felt like a balm cooling my hot skin. The blood had already turned to dust on my sword.

I sheathed the sword. What *was* this creature? He'd said Salem would set him free, but that was all I knew. His whole presence was anathema to me—drought and fire. Water was life. This thing was death.

I glanced at the trees, their leaves blackened and shriveled. Then I stared stupidly down at the pavement, ignoring the humans bustling around me. I barely registered the sound of the sirens wailing as I stared at the ground where the creature had once been.

The way he'd heated the air, wilted the plants... Was this part of Salem's army? Gods have mercy, I could only hope there weren't more of these things coming.

I sheathed my sword again, slipping back into the shadows. Police lights flickered around me. Already humans were bustling around the injured woman, helping her sit up.

Since I wasn't actually a knight, I didn't want to be here when officials started asking awkward questions. Like *who are you,* and *what are you doing with that blood-soaked sword?*

I walked quickly back to the castle, eager to get within its magical protections again before an army of these fire fae showed up—with Salem leading the charge.

2

SALEM

I sniffed the air, smelling smoke. Flames seemed to follow me wherever I went.

I pulled out my alligator-skin flask and took a sip of brandy, letting the sweet flavor roll over my tongue.

I'd been in Jerusalem when the Romans burned it, then again when the crusaders arrived and seared their way through the city, leaving charred bodies in the streets.

Around me, shops selling religious trinkets crammed the narrow street. I stopped to look at one of the displays—a table cluttered with pictures of saints, glittering crystal beads, and the image humans so loved of a man being tortured to death on a cross. For some reason, that brought them comfort.

I leaned over, my eyes on a ceramic figurine of a saint. He held birds in his hands.

The crusaders had come cursing my name, promising to vanquish me. Enemies of *Lucifer*.

I didn't like that name anymore. Lucifer. It meant light-bringer, and I was nearly out of light.

Instead, I'd given the name Lightbringer to my sword—a blade as ancient as the fall itself, hewn from the stars.

I flicked the saint over, and he sent the figurines behind him tumbling.

As I slipped into the crowd again, I ran my fingertip over my sword's iron hilt. If I pulled it from its sheath, celestial flames would dance down the steel. The real Lightbringer. Not me.

In any case, not a single crusader found me on their pilgrimages. They'd left mountains of bodies behind, one faction fighting another. Frankly, I couldn't tell these human tribes apart. They all seemed the same. Angry about books, their stories written in fire and blood.

At least their holy flames had kept me warm, and that was all I needed to know.

I slid through the crowds like smoke. No one seemed to see me unless I wanted them to.

My fingers were on the hilt of my sword again, an old habit.

I'd be sending for Aenor soon, compelling her to come to me. Her impending arrival was stirring something dark in me. I had a feeling she'd awaken some of my most primitive impulses when she was in my complete control. And maybe I liked that thought.

Was that... excitement I felt?

As the narrow market street opened, I glanced up at the sky. My gaze landed on a plume of dark smoke curling above the buildings of the narrow streets. Maybe I'd suppressed the real beast in me, but I couldn't help but move closer to the sound of pain.

Flames and suffering drew me closer, like a magpie to a jewel.

On a narrow road, wedged between shops, a home

burned. From the window, a young auburn-haired woman screamed. Something about her stairs being on fire. Gods, the drama of some people.

I breathed in the scent of smoke, filling my lungs. The woman's shrieks brought a little smile to my lips.

Curiosity got the better of me, and I opened my eyes again, my gaze flicking to her wooden door. I prowled closer to it, pressing a palm against the wood, letting heat surge from my hand. The door ignited, then crumbled to ash.

Fight fire with fire.

As I crossed inside, the smoke curled around me in a wispy embrace. Inside, the building was an inferno. Good thing flames didn't hurt me.

The sound of drums pounded in my blood, a dark and steady beat.

Drums, to drown out the screams of the dying...

The wooden banisters were on fire, and flames lined the edges of the stairs. Soon they'd be ash.

I moved up them quickly, drawn to the sound of shrieking. Screams pierced the air—no drums to drown them out here.

The woman sat on the floor now, soot smudging her white dress and her cheeks. Sweat trickled down her temples.

The fear in her eyes heated something in me. Something from the bad old days... Just a flicker of emotion that sparked and died again.

Perhaps I wanted to see her burn before me. A sacrifice.

Was it pleasure I felt? I wasn't sure, but it was a relief to feel something again, even for a moment.

But instead of watching her burn, something compelled me to cross to her, the floor creaking as I did. In minutes, it could collapse, and she'd be dead.

She reached up for me, arms straining like a child's.

I scooped her up. "I'll bring you down," I said quietly. "Stay calm."

It wasn't a shock that the woman refused to stay calm. Humans rarely did when you asked them to, and often worked against their own best interests.

Instead, she screamed, her nails digging into me, and I carried her down the stairs, shifting her body carefully to avoid catching her clothing in the flames. She began coughing uncontrollably, then buried her face into my chest. She coughed into my sweater. She was in complete hysterics, though I supposed oxygen deprivation did that to a human body. Frail little things.

As I reached the bottom, I heard the wood groan as the stairs tumbled to the floor behind me. Crossing outside, I breathed in the clear air. I tried to put the woman down, but she clung to my neck, her grip like iron. She was still coughing into my chest, about to be sick. I held on to her, no longer as interested in the creature as when she'd been near death. Now she just seemed an irritation.

After a few minutes, her coughing slowed, and I was able to shift her down to stand on the pavement. Still, she gripped onto my mohair sweater.

Soot smudged one of her cheeks, and her green eyes streamed from the smoke. She stared up at me, her mouth slightly open.

"You saved my life." She breathed in deeply, her chest rising and falling. She'd nearly died, and already desire shone in her eyes. But those two things went together, didn't they? Death and lust. "I don't know how to thank you."

Once, her beauty would have sparked something in me, but those days were long gone. Her terror had been a burning ember in my chest, but her desire did nothing for me. I hadn't felt anything in eons. Hadn't dreamt at night. Hadn't desired a woman. Nothing but dead ashes inside.

I pulled my hands from her grasp. "Then it's fortunate I'd rather you didn't thank me."

I turned to walk away from her, following the winding street back to my house.

That had been an interesting diversion, but already, my mind was turning back to the blue-haired morgen.

The beautiful, dethroned princess.

I'd be returning her magic to her. Was it stupid to give her so much power? Perhaps, but she wouldn't keep it long. As soon as she finished what I wanted of her, I'd kill her.

Cold ash lay where my heart used to be. But when I killed Aenor, I'd feel again. Then the spirit of sweet revenge and victory would burn in me like a star.

As I walked, my silhouette cast a long shadow over the walls, and my heart raced. The days were getting shorter, which meant my time was running out. I had only until the Samhain to get what I wanted.

My destiny had a deadline, and if I missed it, I'd be trapped here forever. I had one week left, and I wouldn't miss my one opportunity.

I'd burn the whole world down to get what I wanted.

3

AENOR

I shoved my hands into my skirt pockets as I walked, and the rain started to drench me.

Adrenaline buzzed through my veins as I tried to work out where that fae had come from. The effect he'd had on the world around him wasn't like anything I'd seen before.

Salem will set us free.

If there were more of those things roaming the earth, the world would become an inferno. Salem's inferno.

Whatever happened, I had to stop him.

I hurried along the seawall, sucking in the scent of briny marine air. The ocean air whispered over my skin as I walked along the waterfront. The glistening waves crashing below me. When I glanced out at the ocean waves, I felt a surge of protectiveness. The seas were life, and I'd do whatever I could to keep them safe. If the fire fae roamed the earth, the seas would boil.

I needed answers. Fast. Because when Salem came for me, I'd be under his control.

I was heading back to the place where I'd spent the last week: the library.

~

I SAT IN AN ARCHED ALCOVE, sipping my steaming coffee. Lanterns hanging from the vaulted ceilings cast glowing light over two stories of bookshelves. With all these books, connected by ladders, this place was packed with ancient wisdom. It was just that it was often hard to find what you needed.

On my lap, I flipped through a book about spells. I'd found it just lying there in the alcove, open to a page about a binding collar—a collar that would steal a person's magic forever. It also left them insane, gibbering wrecks, tormented by loss.

Would that work on Salem, I wondered? It seemed tempting.

In any case, the spell book gave me an idea. A different tactic now. I hadn't found Salem's name listed in the chronicles of the ancient fae, or the gods, or the cursed. But when he'd chained me up, Salem had used a strange spell. He'd forced me to taste some kind of fruit. It was delicious, really, sweet and tangy, with a juice that ran down my chin and made my pulse race...

But that wasn't the point. The point was that the fruit had done something, and I wanted to find out what it was. And then I wanted to learn how to kill him.

Having flipped through every page, I closed the book on my lap. Then I found my way to the stack of books about curses. After searching the spines, I selected one labeled *Temptations* and paged through the index. It was hard to discern some kind of pattern in most of these books. Texts in the ancient world didn't adhere to logical systems like alphabetization or grouping by concept. Instead, they could be arranged by "elegance and beauty of the first letters," or other things that made no sense.

I took another sip of coffee, getting a much-needed caffeine jolt.

When I turned the page again, I finally found what I was looking for: a picture of a ripe red piece of fruit hanging from a tree. *Bingo.* My pulse raced. I stared at the fruit a little too long, remembering how delicious it had tasted, my mouth watering.

Mentally, I translated the ancient fae text.

The forbidden fruit of enchantment—a power unique to—

The name was crossed out. It had to be Salem, though. Who else used fruit?

Allows him to track the enchanted.

Another sip of coffee. Tracking. That was what I'd expected. Obviously he knew where I was here in Acre. He could find me wherever I went. That wasn't the worst thing in the world, was it?

I read on.

Gives him the power to compel the enchanted to do whatever he desires. He controls their minds and bodies completely.

Cannot be broken.

My stomach sank.

This was... worse than I'd thought.

Salem had complete power over my mind and body, and I hadn't found any updates on how to kill him.

I leaned back against the window, closing my eyes to try to think clearly.

What had that fire fae said about him?

Salem will set us free. Something about the evening star, and—

Mag Mell. It was an ancient kingdom, I was nearly positive. One of the many fae kingdoms, now lost to time.

I leapt up, spilling a little coffee on myself, and rushed to where I remembered seeing a book about ancient kingdoms.

Fallen king of Mag Mell...

I scanned the shelves, weaving through one stack after another, until I found the words *Mag Mell* inscribed on the spine of an ancient book.

Bingo.

I pulled it from the shelf and started flipping the pages. They were old and water-damaged, the ink smudged, but the book started off clear.

It began with the whole fae history. The heavenly beings in the skies were divided into two broad types: gods and angels. Sometimes, the celestial gods beamed like stars in the heavens.

The evening star. That was what the fire fae called him.

After the heavenly wars, the losing gods and angels fell to earth. They started to change. Most became demons. Some became fae—those who'd fallen to the part of the earth that later became the British Isles. The fae reveled in earthly joys: dancing, sunlight, wine.

And in these ancient days of the early fae, some formed a paradise called Mag Mell.

The following page was *very* interesting. It was about an ancient race of fae called the Fomorians. A picture illustrated a gnarled, flame-headed creature with burning fingertips—exactly like I'd just killed. So *that's* what it was.

Apparently, the first king of Mag Mell had displaced the Fomorians from the land. They were supposed to be extinct. And if they ever returned, they'd bring drought and fires with them wherever they went.

The foul creatures once withered plants and dried the rivers with evil heat. The prophecies say King—— might raise them once more if he is not stopped.

I turned the pages, scanning the history of the Kingdom. My pulse raced as I saw this book, too, had been defaced.

King——, fallen god of twilight, was the second king of Mag Mell. He ruled for centuries. But he was too wicked to reign, and was cast out of the paradise. He roamed the earth, torturing and burning others for his evil pleasure. His true name was struck from the histories, and he remains cursed to this day. Fire follows him wherever he goes.

Some call him the devil, or the dark lord.

The Merrow holds the key to his demise.

A chill spread through my blood like melting ice. The devil?

I pulled out another stick of wintergreen, popping it in my mouth. It didn't taste great with the coffee.

At least I had a clue now. *The Merrow holds the key...*

I read on.

Only one person can vanquish him for good.

The Merrow. The next page was streaked by water damage, and I could only make out a few words. *Sinful... lustful... sexual depravity... he torments...*

I cleared my throat, straightening.

The Merrow was my answer, and it just so happened that I knew him. He'd been in Ys many times. I could still remember the sound of his powerful magic. Once, I'd helped him with a powerful spell, back when Mama was still alive. He'd captured a monster in driftwood cages, and I'd helped him sink it to the bottom of the sea.

The plan was crystalizing now, though there wasn't much to it.

I had to lead Salem to the Merrow.

Footfalls had me jumping, and I turned to see Lyr crossing toward me. Between the stacks, shadows breathed around him. His expression was grim.

I let out a long sigh of relief, closing the book. "Where have you been? I haven't seen you in days. Apparently, Salem is the devil himself. Lucifer. And he can control my mind."

Lyr's body glowed gold, and for the first time, I realized he was dripping wet, his dark eyelashes frozen together in little peaks. "I've been with Beira."

The Winter Witch. He put all his faith in that Winter Witch. "What did she say?"

"You are the only one who can kill him, according to Beira. You have to stop him from trying to fulfill his destiny. If you fail, the whole world will turn to ash."

4

AENOR

L yr held out his hand, opening his fist. A white pearl gleamed in his palm. "This contains the prophecy from Beira. Put it in your mouth, and you will see what will happen if you don't kill Salem."

"I don't need the extra motivation."

Still, I plucked the pearl from his palm. With a nervous look up at him, I popped it in my mouth.

Immediately, the book stacks and arched ceilings around me gave way to a forest of blazing trees. Tree trunks burned like torches, and heat scorched my skin. A woman ran across the flaming landscape, her body on fire. Her cries tore through the air, and her body flailed around.

A creature—just like the one I'd killed earlier—loped through the forest, fingers flaming. Steam curled off his gnarled body.

It felt like I stood on the surface of the sun, the air so dry and hot...

I tried to remind myself that this was only a vision, a possibility... but right now, it all seemed so real.

I couldn't breathe for all the smoke, and the heat

scorched my skin. I blinked as flames curled around me, and I ran. I was trying to find a way out of this inferno. A path cut through the woods, leading to a road. Coughing, I tried to run as fast as possible, desperate for clear air. When I reached the highway, I found a sea of wrecked cars, people running, bodies in flames, cars exploding...

Salem will do this...

The vision ripped from my mind, and I stared instead at Lyr standing before me.

My knees had gone weak, nearly buckling, and I reached out for him.

It was only a vision, and yet sweat dripped down my forehead. My skin felt like it had been scorched. It took a moment for the heat to fade.

I caught my breath. Lyr had seemed to flinch when I'd reached for him, and I stepped away again.

Since Lyr had brought me back from the dead, he seemed... different. Like another part of him had stayed in the death realm.

The fact that he didn't want me to touch him made my heart twist.

"That vision was bleak," I rasped. "And believe me, I want to kill him anyway. I've been meaning to kill him for a long time."

"There's a particular shard of enchanted sea glass we need to use, but she wasn't clear on where to get it."

The Merrow. He was supposed to be the key. "Okay, I have good news and I have bad news. The bad news is that the fruit I ate means Salem can control my mind. Killing him won't be super easy."

Lyr growled, low and deep, the sound rumbling through my belly. "I'll help you find the sea glass. We'll kill him together."

"But here's the good news. The books said that the Merrow holds the key to his demise. So maybe that's the sea glass. I can lure Salem to the Merrow. The Merrow traps him, and I stab him."

Lyr's eyes narrowed. "Didn't you tell me Salem wanted to return your power to you?"

At the thought of it, my mood brightened. "That's the other good news. With my sea power back, I should be able to find the Merrow."

Lyr shook his head. "No, we can't allow this to happen. If Salem controls your mind, he controls your power. He could do untold damage. I'll help you trap him as soon as he arrives to get you. Then we'll get the Merrow."

Instantly, I balked at this idea, but it took me a moment to figure out why. "If we trap him as soon as he arrives, I will never get my power back."

"And the world will be safer."

I pinched the bridge of my nose. "First of all, the loss of my power is like missing my limbs. If you'd lost an integral part of yourself, and you had the chance to get it back, you would take it. Second of all, I think only the Merrow can trap him. Beira said I'm the only one who can kill him. But the Merrow is the one who can trap him. The Merrow holds the key."

He ran his thumb over his lip, seeming to consider this for a moment. "How do you know about this trapping?"

"I've helped him do it before. He can trap a person's soul in an old driftwood cage, tethering their body and spirit to the spot. Long ago, we buried someone under the ocean waters. If I can bring Salem to him, we can trap him long enough for me to find this sea glass. I think the Merrow and I have to work together."

Lyr's brow furrowed. "You've done this before?"

"Long ago, when I had my power. It was an evil fae of astounding powers. He was going to destroy Ys and turn it into dust and ash. It was... it was exactly like the vision you just showed me. The same exact thing. If we hadn't trapped him, everything would have burned. I saw it using my own magic. I used to call them *what if* spells. What if I don't trap this person? And it was just fire and drought everywhere. Smoldering rock, bodies lying in rubble across our island. So I helped the Merrow. We stopped the world from burning."

"The Winter Witch said nothing about this Merrow."

"Well, she tends to leave out important details."

He fell silent for a long moment, and I felt like an icy gulf had opened between us. "She cautioned me against you."

"Against *me?*" That frigid chasm opened even further. I crossed my arms. "The Winter Witch cautioned you against me? Why, exactly?"

"She warned that your magic is a threat to the world. She believes you're mentally unstable."

"Don't you think in a world that's on fire, someone who can control ice and water might be an asset? Look, I'm certain that Salem is trying to find a way to bring the Fomorians back."

He sighed. "They don't exist anymore."

"It was in the freaking vision you just showed me. Didn't you see it in the vision?"

He shook his head. "No, it wasn't in the vision."

Frustration simmered. Why hadn't he seen it? "I killed one today."

"That's impossible. They were defeated tens of thousands of years ago."

I grabbed his arms. "The thing was right out by the

seawall. He scorched the trees and all the rain was evaporating. If I have my powers back, I can fight them."

He arched an eyebrow, pulling his arms from my grasp. "If you killed one, show me the body."

I wasn't insane. He was trying to make me think I was insane, but I wasn't. "He disappeared after I killed him."

A heavy silence. "It was probably something else. Look, unless you're a god or completely pure of heart, the amount of power you once wielded could corrupt someone completely."

Coldness spread across my heart. A distance had crept between us like long shadows. "You still don't trust me. You trust the Winter Witch more than me."

"It would be dangerous for *anyone* to have that much power. It troubled you before. You told me that's why you drank so much."

My hands tightened into fists. "Things were too bright, and too loud. I felt things too intensely with my magic. That's why I had a lot of wine. But I never did anything terrible."

He lifted his other fist, and when he unfurled his fingers, he revealed another pearl. This one gleamed black. "And yet this is what happens if you are allowed to keep your powers."

I stared down at it. I was so close to getting back my magic now, within a hummingbird's breath of it. Restoration to my former greatness, within my grasp.

And the Winter Witch was about to poison it all.

And what if she was lying, or mad? Or just *wrong*?

I glared at it. "I get the idea. My sea magic is scary. But I don't need to see this vision, which is just a possibility—"

Lyr stepped forward so swiftly that I didn't have time to react, and he cupped the side of my head.

Another vision slammed into my mind—a flooded world with chunks of ice floating in the sea. My sea magic shimmered over a frozen landscape, and my mind whirled. Behind me, knights stood frozen, icicles glinting from their beards.

I smacked Lyr's hands away, and the vision disappeared. "Stop it. I need you to trust me. I'm not going to lose my mind and drown the world in ice."

"I know you wouldn't. But Salem might, while controlling you."

He had a point, but I wasn't willing to give this up so easily. "That doesn't jibe with his fire plans, does it?" I exhaled sharply. "Anyway, what if I can learn to resist it? I can practice with Melisande's enchantment."

He stepped away from me, and shadows seemed to swallow him. "I'll see what else I can find out from Beira. Then we can try resisting enchantment with Melisande."

Beira, again. He *definitely* trusted her more than he trusted me, even though she was batshit.

He turned and walked away from me, crossing out of the library into the castle's dark hall. As I watched him go, loneliness ate at my chest.

5

AENOR

In the great hall, I sat across from Gwydion. He grinned at me over his wine, the torchlight dancing over his dark skin. "The knights and I vanquished an entire vampire army south of here today. And what did you accomplish? A half-baked plan to resist the devil?"

I grabbed the bottle of dandelion wine for myself. "I have bigger issues than vampire armies to worry about. Apparently, Gwydion, the fate of the world lies in my hands."

"I heard. Sounds to me like we're all completely fucked." He shrugged. "You do know the spell, don't you? You can summon us to wherever you are once you screw everything up."

"I have it memorized. Lyr had me repeat it ten thousand times."

"Good. Well, I'm just here for the show with Melisande. Not that I particularly care to see her force you to smash your head against the wall again. I mean, it was funny at the time, but I don't know. A little gauche, perhaps?"

"Not exactly the word I'd use, but it's a start."

"Speaking of gauche, does it bother you that Melisande and Lyr used to rut like animals years ago?"

"Like I said. Bigger issues on my mind." I sipped my wine. "But any animals in particular?"

He let out a dramatic sigh. "It's not fun if it doesn't make you jealous. You know, I once cursed an ex-lover to grow a horse's tail after I caught him looking too long at a human simpleton." He twirled the stem of his wineglass. "Speaking of human simpletons, what happened to yours?"

Gina was no simpleton. She was back in London, applying to colleges. "None of your business."

The sound of clanking chains heralded Melisande's arrival, and I turned to see her walking through the hall behind Lyr, hands bound.

Despite her time in prison, she still managed to look gorgeous, her skin glowing and dark hair cascading over her shoulders.

She hissed at me. "You cut my wings off, Aenor."

"And you betrayed your own court and tried to kill me." I smiled sweetly. "You're lucky I left you alive."

She blew a strand of dark hair out of her eyes. "Well, my wings are growing back. I'll work my way back into the court's good graces. And I didn't need to kill you because you're dead inside. I can see it in your eyes. *Dead.*"

My pulse raced.

"Melisande," Lyr cut in sharply. "You're here for one reason and one reason alone. We're going to see if Aenor can resist a mind-control enchantment."

"This will be fun." Gwydion grinned.

"Why?" asked Melisande. "What stupid shit's she got herself into now?"

"You don't need to know that." Lyr pinned me with his pale gaze. "Aenor, this is only a test. But you need to imagine a protective bubble in your mind. It's like a clear bubble that pushes out another person's influence. Close your eyes and picture it, clear as you can."

I nodded, closing my eyes. In my mind's eye, I envisioned a bubble of shining white light, a crystalline surface. I opened my eyes, keeping the mental image. "All right, Melisande. Hit me with your magic."

"Wait." Lyr grabbed her arm. "You do understand that you can't do anything that hurts her, right? Just enchant her to do something harmless. No injuries."

"Boring. But fine," she snapped, and she stared into my eyes.

I summoned a clear bubble in my thoughts, but as soon as Melisande's eyes began shifting to warm hues, my mental bubble started to melt.

How could I resist the goddess standing before me? She beamed like the sun.

I fell hard to my knees, grinning up at her. There was something I was supposed to be doing now, but it was hard to remember, because I had to worship her.

She snatched the bottle of wine off the table, then handed it to me.

I took it from her, grinning. A gift from a goddess!

"Pour it on yourself, tunnel swine," she said.

How was I to resist her charm?

I poured out the whole bottle on my head, dousing myself in sweet dandelion wine. It streamed down my hair and face, soaking my shirt, just like she wanted. I licked my lips, tasting its delicious tang.

"Now, from your knees, tell me about how you're a filthy little mud whore," she said.

"That's enough." Lyr's barked words broke the spell as Melisande's gaze snapped away from me.

I looked down at my wine-soaked tank top and shorts. *Ugh.*

"This obviously isn't working," said Lyr.

"Let me try again," I snapped. "It was just my first try."

This *had* to work.

Lyr's pale hair whipped around his head as his magic whirled around him. He looked furious.

"Fine, Aenor. Try again. *Focus.* If you are unable to do this, we can't allow Salem to return your power to you."

I took a deep breath and rose from where I kneeled. I squeezed out the wine from my tank top onto the stone floor. "I can do this."

Clear bubble, like a sphere of air in the wide ocean.

I shook out my limbs like an athlete getting ready for a race. Then I closed my eyes, calling to mind a shiny glass sphere. In my mind's eye, I gave it a pearly sheen—so real I could almost touch it.

"Okay," I said.

Melisande's eyes shifted to the color of flames, and my breath caught in my throat.

The bubble gleamed in my mind, and I pushed out the feel of her magic, blocked out her influence. She was talking to me, but I wasn't going to listen this time. I was Aenor Dahut of Meriadoc, Scourge of the Wicked, and I would resist. This time, I would prove that...

This time...

What was I doing?

Thing was, the goddess before me wanted me to dance on the table. Who was I to argue with a divine being?

Smiling, I leapt onto the table, my hips gyrating to an invisible beat. It was like I could almost hear Elvis floating through the air.

"Stop!" Lyr shouted.

The spell broke.

Son of a gun.

Gwydion smirked. "Was that what humans call twerking?"

Lyr, on the other hand, didn't find this funny at all. His muscles had gone rigid, and his eyes had shifted to gold. When I looked into them deeply, he looked... haunted.

My heart clenched.

I felt like I was disappointing him.

Swallowing hard, I leapt down from the table. "Look, it's just like anything else, I'm sure. It will take practice. I've only tried twice, and that one was a little better. So we'll just try again. We can keep trying, until I'm good at it." My wine-soaked top clung to my skin. "Just give me a second to clear my thoughts again."

But as I started to call up my clear bubble, a raven swooped into the room. My pulse raced at the sight of a tiny piece of paper in its beak. Another message from Salem.

Circling above my head, the raven opened its beak, and the scrap of paper fluttered to the ground. I picked it up and read it, my heart hammering.

Walk outside to meet my driver now. He will take you to Jerusalem. Don't try to resist, pet. I control you now.

Tick tock. Time was up.

6

AENOR

L yr took the paper from me, his body glowing with magical light as he read it. "No. We're not delivering you to him so he can control your power. It's like we're giving him a powerful weapon."

"Does she have a choice?" asked Gwydion. "Beira said this wine-soaked wretch is supposed to save the world. The books say the Merrow plays a part. She'll have to get to Salem to make that happen, and he's not here. He sent a driver. Look, Lyr, a prophecy is a prophecy."

"Stop talking, Gwydion," Lyr snarled. "Before I rip your heart out."

Lyr had shifted into his Ankou form, horns gleaming tall on his head. He liked to be in control, and he wasn't in control of any of this.

He glared at his brother. "Seneschal, take our prisoner back to the dungeons."

Gwydion grunted, then started dragging Melisande out by her chained hands. Melisande shot me one last furious look before she skulked away behind the seneschal.

Now, Lyr and I were completely alone in the shadowy hall.

"Just trust me, Lyr," I said. "I can do this. I've memorized the summoning spell if I really need you."

I felt that icy gulf again between us. I didn't want to reach for him again only to find him stepping away.

"What is going on with you?" I hadn't realized I was about to say it before the words were out of my mouth.

For just a second, his determined features softened. Then wildness burned in his eyes.

"I have a new plan," he said. "I know a way that we can stop your magic. We kill this servant that he has sent. We hang the driver's body from the castle. We bring Salem to us, then I trap him. We trap him forever. Then you can return to London, and things will be just like they were before."

For one dreadful moment, I felt like the world was shaking underneath me, that a wave of water was about to swallow me up. This was a freaking punch to the gut, wasn't it?

"You want me to return to London?"

His brow furrowed. "Things need to return to the way they were. So I can have my mind back. You said you had no interest in ruling Nova Ys. Is that still the case?"

"Yes, but that's not..." That wasn't what was hurting my heart. "You want things to return to how they were before we knew each other."

Salem's lackey was waiting right outside for me, and this was what Lyr decided to say? *I want you to leave.*

"You cost me a part of my soul," he said quietly.

"I'm sorry." I didn't know what to say, but it wasn't like I'd done it on purpose.

His gaze cleared. "Look, we don't have time for this. We

will kill Salem's servant, and then I will block your power. I have a binding collar that I can put around your neck."

"*What?*" So that was why the book had been open in the library. Lyr had been researching how to steal my power for good.

That haunted look returned to his eyes, his pupils going unfocused. "A collar. It will dampen or eradicate any magical power you might acquire. It will help to mitigate the risk in case Salem manages to get his hands on you."

"I know what it is, but no. *Hells* no."

He stepped closer, body tense. "You saw the risk. Fields torched, crops on fire. People burning in the streets, smoke rising from their bodies. Charred corpses. You can't give him more power. We kill Salem, together. Nothing else matters. Then it can all go back to the way it was before."

Before we ever met.

He held out his open palm, and a small ring glowed in it. The ring expanded, till it was large enough to fit around a person's neck. The binding collar.

"Once this is on you," he said, "you won't even see it. Or feel it."

At that moment, I felt the ghost of my sea magic start to whisper up my spine, making me shiver. My stolen magic was calling to me like a lost child.

Instinct compelled me to step away from Lyr. He took another step closer, and I found that phantom yearning for my magic intensifying. It was a sharp ache between my ribs. "No. And your plan doesn't even make sense."

Gold light beamed around Lyr's body, tingling across my skin.

I could almost imagine them, the claws of ice that would sprout from my fingertips... "I'm not the threat, Lyr. It's the Fomorians. The fire fae. They will make the seas boil. They will destroy all life on earth by heating the air. I can stop them. I'm the one who can stop them." The words tumbled out of my mouth, and I realized how nuts I sounded.

Lyr cocked his head, eyes gleaming. He didn't believe a word I was saying.

Suddenly, I *wanted* to get out of here. I wanted to run and never look back.

I focused on the feel of my feet on the stone ground, trying to root myself to the earth.

I have survived. I will keep surviving.

I'd been through worse, hadn't I? I'd lived a hundred and fifty years looking after myself.

I glanced at the collar in his hand again, my thoughts whirling so fast that I could hardly think straight. "I can do this, Lyr. I can find a way to manipulate Salem. He wants me to find something for him, and I'll lead him to the Merrow. Understand this: I've wanted to kill him for a hundred years, long before I even knew his name. He ruined my life." I thought of what Melisande had said: *dead inside.* "Over a century, I've wanted to kill him. This is my chance to get my power back, and to get my revenge. And save the world. Like Beira said. This is my destiny, and I've never felt something so strongly before in my life."

As soon as the words were out of my mouth, another raven swooped in with a piece of paper in its beak. I held out my shaking hand, and the raven dropped the paper. It fluttered into my palm.

Leave now, or face my wrath, Aenor. I'm not a patient man.

Lyr pulled it out of my hand. "He will feel my wrath when I rip his driver's head from his body."

"I don't think that will achieve much of anything. I doubt the devil cares for his driver."

I was about to head back to my room for my things when Salem's wrath arrived.

It started with a sound like a drumbeat in my mind. A deep, slow rhythm pounding through my blood, a beat echoing off rocky cave walls.

A dark heartbeat, and a voice from the oldest parts of my brain—the command of a primal god.

Pick up the wine bottle. Smash it.

My own thoughts rebelled. This wasn't like Melisande's enchantment. I was still here, still trying to resist. And yet I found myself pulling away from Lyr and spinning around to snatch the wine bottle from the middle of the table. I brought it down hard on the wood tabletop, shattering the end to leave jagged edges of glass.

Panic filled my lungs.

Press the broken shards to your wrist.

Even as my own mind screamed, I felt myself pressing the shattered end to my wrist—

Lyr caught my arms, pulling them apart. He squeezed my wrist hard enough that the broken bottle dropped to the floor, shattering completely, then he pulled me close against him, dragging me away from the table, away from the wine bottle. For the first time in days, I was in a tight embrace.

But I didn't feel any warmth from it. All I felt was Salem watching me, waiting to see if I'd follow his orders. Seemed he didn't even have to be here to control me.

"You're not ready to go yet," Lyr snapped.

"I clearly don't have a choice." And I wanted to go, too. It was like the past hundred and forty years had suddenly crystalized into a single purpose: kill my nemesis.

I tried pulling away from the tight embrace, but Lyr suddenly didn't seem to want to let me go. He held tight to my arm, then lifted the collar before my face. It gleamed pale blue.

"Let go of me," I snarled.

"And let you be Salem's plaything?"

I bristled at the term *plaything.*

"It's for your own protection," he went on. "I know you'd never forgive yourself if Salem made you kill millions of people."

Oh, he was *good.*

I actually considered it for a moment. Then I glanced down at the collar, repulsed by its metallic sheen. "It doesn't add up. The prophecy is fire. Not ice or water."

Was it Salem that Lyr feared so much—or me? Why did I feel like this was punishment for the loss of his soul?

Lyr rolled the collar in his hands, the movements hypnotic. The rest of his body stayed completely still. A chill rippled over my skin, adrenaline pulsing. Instinct told me to hold on to my power as much as I could, that I'd need it. That it was the best way to fight the real threat of the Fomorians.

His eyes blazing with gold, Lyr reached for me with the collar—

My stomach swooped. That was when I yanked my arm from his grip and ran at full speed. I ran for the window, arms flailing.

I felt the water calling for me, asking for me to keep it safe.

And I leapt for the sea.

7

AENOR

W hen I hit the water, something felt wrong in the sea. I couldn't quite make out what it was, though. With a pang of regret, I realized I hadn't had enough time to grab my comb—my own tool of enchantment.

Still, I didn't have time to mull over any of that now. Lyr and every knight in the fortress would be after me within moments, wielding that damn collar.

I kicked my legs, propelling myself through the cold water with the stunning speed of a morgen. The knights would be after me, but I had an advantage in the water.

After swimming a few minutes, I could hear them following behind me, the vibrations of their magic pulsing through the waves. My stomach clenched. How quickly I'd become their enemy.

Lyr had lost his damn mind, but at least I could run from him. His World Key wasn't much use if he didn't know where to find me.

Salem, on the other hand, was someone I couldn't run from. Not yet.

I swam faster, blood pounding as I rushed through the water. I didn't stray far from the shoreline, hugging it as I swam south along the coast.

Slowly, it started to dawn on me what was wrong with the sea around me.

It was ever so slightly too hot. Just a degree or two. I wasn't sure how I could tell, but it just felt warmer than it should be. Had that single Fomorian been able to change it so fast?

As I swam, I heard the drumbeat in my mind again. Salem, watching me, wherever I went. With that sinister rhythm pounding over my skin, I felt an overwhelming desire to turn and head for the shore.

As the drum pounded through my blood, I called to mind the image of a clear bubble. Except Salem's magic seemed to be about sound, and the image in my mind did nothing to keep it out. Inside my mind, I imagined a song, trying to drown out the drumbeat for just a moment—

But his magic boomed louder, and I found myself compelled to turn for the shore, moving at a fast clip.

I'd done it, though, for just a moment. I'd started to resist him.

When I stepped out onto the shoreline, the first thing I saw was a Lincoln Town Car parked by the street, windows shaded black. Already, I knew it belonged to Salem.

I glanced behind me, my breath stuttering at the sight of Gwydion coming for me, sword drawn. Lyr strode from the sea right behind him. He gripped the binding collar.

Fear tightened my throat, and I rushed for the car like Salem was my salvation. I wrenched open the rear door, throwing myself into the back seat. One last glance at the sea, and I saw them running for me at full speed.

"Drive!" I shouted.

I hadn't even had a chance to get a look at the driver when the car pulled out at shocking speed. I slammed back into the leather seats, scrambling to right myself. As the driver took a sharp turn, I grasped frantically for the seatbelt. He was leaning on the gas with frightening aggression, but I guessed the situation called for it.

A magical attack spell slammed into the car, and I hit the seat in front of me before I could get the belt on. *Gods, are they going to kill us?*

I tumbled again as the driver took a sharp turn, smacking against the door. As the driver sped around yet another corner, I managed to grab hold of a seatbelt and jam it into place with the full force of my will.

I turned, looking through the rear window. Distantly, I saw the crackle of magic through the streets. Still, we'd lost them.

It was at this point that I smelled the air, which was thick with marijuana. For the first time, I glanced at the driver.

In the front seat was a large, slender fae gripping the wheel, with a spliff hanging out of his mouth. The streetlights flickered over him as he sped past them, and I could see that he wore a crooked crown of dandelions threaded into his messy platinum curls.

"Aenor," he said. "You made this pickup harder than it needed to be, you know. Ruined my chill vibe in here."

He wasn't wearing a shirt. Over his arms and chest, names were tattooed. Women's names—*Amy, Zenobia, Laura...*

In the front seat, near his head, three colored birds flitted around. By their glittering sheen, I could tell they were magic. As we sped past another car, their wings flapped frantically.

The stranger turned to look at me, still driving at an

insane speed, eyes not even on the road. When the street-lights flashed on his irises, I saw pale grey streaked with gold. His lips curled in a half-smile. He was pretty, really. "Glad you made it, though. I was a little worried I might have to kill everyone in the castle and ruin my buzz."

He turned around again and careened onto an exit that took us onto a highway. I still felt too stunned to speak. From the car speakers, a hip-hop song about donuts played softly.

Not what I expected, but okay.

"What's your name?" I asked.

"Ossian. Your driver. I'm not normally a driver, you know, on account of I don't entirely know how to drive. It doesn't seem that hard, though, you know what I mean? And I'm a fast learner. I didn't want to tell Salem I couldn't drive, because, you know... It didn't feel manly. So I just went with it." He shrugged. "You got your seatbelt on, yeah? I'm supposed to bring you alive."

"I do now." I lowered my face into my hands, trying not to think about what the hells had just happened.

"You look sad, girl," said Ossian. "Tell me what happened. Do I need to fuck somebody up?"

"Oh, are we going to talk?"

"I sense heartbreak. I've got a knack for sensing it. It's my thing."

I nearly launched into the whole story about Lyr, before remembering that Ossian was taking me into captivity with a monster. "Well, for one thing, you're delivering me to the devil. Any idea what he wants?"

"Revenge, I think?"

I blinked. "Against me? For what, exactly? Not dying easily enough when he destroyed my kingdom?"

"Nah... Something else. Anyway, I can't really get into that. He just needs you to help him find something. So the real question is, who broke your heart? Because I will fuck him up."

I fell silent, my mind turning over the word *revenge.* I felt hollow.

"Was it the big blond one coming after us?" he added. "Looked like a proper dickhead, if you ask me."

"I didn't."

"You're well rid of that *wanker.* Trust me." Smoke clouded around him.

I sighed, resigned to this conversation. "What makes you an expert, then?"

"Oh, I know heartbreak, believe me."

"So are we going to be bonding over pints of ice cream and wine coolers sometime soon?"

"I wouldn't rule it out, my friend. As long as you stay alive. Because honestly, I'm not sure what Salem has planned for you."

I rubbed my eyes. "You seem very concerned for the state of my love life considering your total disregard for my *actual* life."

"Well, you know, I've come to accept I can't control everything." He spoke with a London accent. "Fate rules us all, innit."

I guessed it wouldn't kill me to make an ally. "So who broke your heart, then?"

"Fate," he barked, suddenly energized. "Fate broke my heart."

I pinched the bridge of my nose. "What happened, Ossian?"

"What's the worst thing that can happen to a fae? Do you know? Guess."

"I don't know. Losing your kingdom and your magic comes to mind, but I'm sure there are worse scenarios. Children dying? Being tortured to death? I'm sorry, this is the most morbid guessing game I've ever played. I will be needing that ice cream soon. Or vodka."

"I'll tell you, Aenor. Watching your *mate* die is the worst thing that can happen to a fae. You don't have a mate, do you?" He took a hit from his spliff. "If you did, you wouldn't have been running from that proper dickhead."

"No, no mate for me." To be honest, I'd never been sure if fated mates were real or not.

"They're rare. Very rare. But here's the thing: if you find your mate, you are driven to protect them at all costs. You no longer care about your own life so much. You only care about theirs. As long as your mate is okay, you're happy."

A feeling of dread rose in my stomach at where this story was going. "And something happened to yours?"

"Ripped apart by the Ollephest," he said quietly. "I saw it happen."

Brutal. "I'm so sorry."

The Ollephest was a terrifying sea dragon I hoped never to encounter. Phantomlike, it could sneak up on you unnoticed. It got inside your head. The first sign that it was nearby was that your worst fears seemed to manifest before you, and you could no longer tell what was real or what was imagined.

Then, while you were hallucinating and flailing, it would solidify into a serpent form and eat you alive.

"Her name was Willow. We were sailing in the Irish Sea, heading for Mag Mell. I mean, she was sailing—I was making music, sunning myself. Strange thing was, I saw her die in my mind first. Because that was my worst fear, wasn't it? I didn't know I was having a vision from the Ollephest. I just thought she stood before me and plunged a knife into her own heart. So I was screaming and screaming..."

The rawness in his voice actually brought tears to my eyes.

He cleared his throat. "Anyway, once the vision dissipated, all I saw was the Ollephest, gnawing on her limbs. Blood coming down his teeth. Her head was..." He fell silent, and I looked out the window. "Sorry, I'm a bit of a downer. Anyway, that was almost two hundred years ago, and I'm not quite over it."

"I'm sorry," I said again.

Better not to have a mate, really, if you risked losing your mind.

His birds swooped around the front seat. "I've done things since then, passed the time. I can make ocean waves. Slept with a lot of women. That kind of thing."

"Wait, ocean waves? You have true sea magic?" I tried to ignore the raging jealousy crashing through my chest.

"I can make a wave. That's it. I could drown a fishing village. I wouldn't, mind you. That'd be mean, and I haven't got anything against fishermen."

I could hardly breathe for all the weed smoke in the car.

"Can you tell me where we're going?" I asked, trying to change the subject.

He blew out circles of smoke. "We drive to the devil's house in Jerusalem. He'll interrogate you there. Then you have to pass a magical test or he'll probably kill you."

Revenge. Against me. I needed to know why.

"Do you know anything about the Fomorians?" I asked.

"The Fomorians? Yeah," he said. "Extinct."

"So I keep hearing, and yet... you've never heard Salem talk about them?"

"Look, Aenor, I don't really know his secrets. And if I did, I wouldn't share them with you." He turned up the music. "I like this song."

I kicked off my shoes, leaning back in my seat. He'd stocked the car with drinks, including mini bottles of wine. I pulled out a bottle of *French Wine* and unscrewed it, drinking straight from the bottle. Not the best, but drinkable.

I stared out the window at the dark highway. "Let's go back to this revenge idea—"

"No, Aenor. I can't tell you all that."

"I thought we were getting to know each other so well. Ice cream and heartbreak and all that."

"I'm starting to think this ride might better if you went to sleep."

I snorted. "I'm not going to sl—"

A magical wave of slumber washed over me before I could finish my sentence, and I dreamt of floating on a soft bed in a lake of glittering water.

8

AENOR

When I woke, I was staring up into Ossian's face. He blinked and pushed a blond curl out of his eyes. His colorful birds fluttered around his head.

What had just happened? I rubbed my eyes, trying to clear the dreams from my mind. Slowly, it dawned on me that I was lying on a cold tile floor. Barrel-vaulted sandstone ceilings arched over me.

So *this* must be Salem's digs.

"She's awake now," Ossian called out.

I pushed up onto my elbows, looking around. I was lying in the middle of a large hall. Alcoves set into the walls displayed vases and urns decorated with ancient alphabets. Lanterns cast golden light over rows of leather-bound books on one wall.

Not far from me, three towering windows overlooked an enclosed garden, bathed in moonlight. A mahogany desk stood against the windows, crystal decanters on its surface.

Apparently, Salem had very good taste. This looked like

a palace, one with a seamless blend of the old and the new. But where was the old bastard?

A movement in the shadows caught my eye, but it was only a black cat. She pranced over then rubbed against me, her eyes beaming with gold. A gold star hung from a silky collar around her neck. As I leaned down to stroke her, she purred loudly. She was powerfully built, muscular for a cat. For one insane moment, I thought she might transform into Salem.

Footfalls turned my head.

He stalked into the room, shadows sweeping behind him like wings. I felt his power from here, malign and ancient, pounding through my blood.

Anticipation danced up my spine at the sight of him, and I rose to stand. My still-damp clothes clung to my body, and I folded my arms in front of my chest.

His dark beauty was like a blade in my heart, the warm light sculpting sharp cheekbones. He smiled, slow and sensual, but there was no warmth in it.

Over his expensive charcoal-colored clothing, he wore a sword slung around his waist, the hilt a beautiful obsidian. And his suit clothed a powerful, muscular body.

The black cat rushed to him, weaving between his legs as he walked. Her purring grew louder.

"Aenor. How good of you to come." As Salem drew closer, I realized now that, like the sunset itself, his eyes changed colors—shifting from a serene, dusky blue to lurid fire. Mesmerizing, really.

His hot magic skimmed over my body, warming me. And yet the malice he exuded made my blood run cold all the same.

I shifted, trying to look relaxed as he closed the distance

between us, peering down at me. His eyes twinkled. I delighted him somehow.

Then he crossed past me, heading for his desk. He leaned against it, smiling faintly. A pulse of dark power radiated off his muscled body—a warning. It felt *evil,* tinged with an undercurrent of pain and sadness.

It took me a moment to realize Ossian had left the room altogether. That made me a little nervous. Ossian had felt vaguely like an ally.

"Why am I here?" I began. "I hear you're the devil. Flattering that you've taken such an interest in me. Shouldn't you be jabbing your pitchfork into people instead? You must be very busy."

"You're mistaken." His eyes danced with fire, but his body looked completely relaxed—a louche king in his domain. "It's a trident, not a pitchfork, and I already filled my quota for the day. There's something you must understand, now. You are in my control." That delight again, twinkling in his eyes. "Last time we met, you were able to enchant me. I've taken pains to ensure you can't wield the same power over me again. I control you now. Understood? Mind and body. You are now my little pet."

My lip curled. "Your *what?*"

"That's what you are, isn't it? *Mine.*" A dark edge imbued the last word.

My blood roared. Let him think he was in control. I'd find a way to fight back. I always did. And while I figured things out, I'd keep quiet.

He rolled up his shirt sleeves, revealing tattoos on his arms. One of them was a winged woman, her figure curved. A star shone above her head. A goddess, maybe?

"Now, little pet," he murmured. "Tell me all about a crime you committed long ago."

This was where I'd find out what I did to him, I supposed. "I've been killing bad guys for over a century. I've cut out thousands of hearts. You'll have to be more specific."

He cocked his head, his eyes now blazing. "How charming. Now cast your mind back to the day you drowned a powerful fae somewhere in the seas. A fae as powerful as I am." The quiet way he spoke disturbed me, like he was trying to force me to move closer to hear him.

It also felt like the calm before a storm.

"You used your power to bury someone under the sea long ago," he added.

"I remember," I said. It was all coming together, wasn't it? The Merrow, the Fomorians... "My memories from those days are a little hazy, but I remember. I had a good reason." Understanding slowly dawned. "Was it you, by any chance? Did you get out, and this is your revenge? I've heard a rumor you don't like me very much."

"I like you very much under my control, but that's about it. What shall I do with you, Aenor?" His silky voice skimmed my body.

I straightened. "Was it you? Is that what this is all about?"

He shook his head slowly, and his sensual smile took on a more sinister curl. "No, not me. The person you drowned is still there, still tormented. You did that."

I swallowed hard. So that was what this was all about. "You want me to find him?"

Amusement danced in his eyes. "Are you leading this interrogation, or am I?"

"This is the interrogation?" I asked. "I'm just standing here. I thought a man with your reputation would be a bit more brutal. No electrocuted nipples?"

His gaze flicked down to my breasts for a second. "Is that

disappointment in your voice? I'm sure it could be arranged, if you really desire it."

My cheeks heated. *Honestly.* Why couldn't I have said earlobes?

"No thanks, I'm trying to cut down," I said brightly, forcing a smile. "So who was this person, then?"

"And there you go again, leading the interrogation." He arched an eyebrow.

His piercing gaze now gave him the look of a predator sizing up prey. "But I am most curious, Aenor. You don't know who you trapped, and yet you did it anyway?" Shadows slid through his eyes. "Seems wantonly sadistic."

Of the many things I had expected when I woke up this morning, being accused of sadism by the devil was not high on the list.

"They wouldn't tell me the man's name," I said. "Only that he wanted to destroy Ys, and perhaps more. I don't always trust other people's prophecies, but I did my own spell. A *what if* spell. They've never been wrong. And I saw what would happen if I hadn't helped bury this fae. Charred bodies would have filled the streets of Ys. Life would have died in the ocean around us. Which brings me to another point—are you trying to raise the Fomorians?"

"Do not try to distract me, pet." His voice was a sharp blade. "You have seen that I can control your mind, and I will the second I need to. I will punish your insolence if I must, and I will enjoy doing it."

I bit my lip, an idea already forming in my mind. On the one hand, I didn't want to lead him to this driftwood cage. If I did, Salem and the imprisoned fae could burn the world down together, or whatever he had planned.

On the other hand, I had to get him to the Merrow. What if I made him think this was all his idea? I just needed

Salem to think he was extracting this idea from me against my will.

I clenched my jaw, giving him a resolute look. "I'm not telling you how to find this friend of yours. I'm certain destruction will only follow. I've seen it. You're going to try to burn the world."

"Aaah, Aenor..." His voice was a seductive breeze that wrapped around my body. "The princess still thinks she's in charge. How delightful it will be when you realize the truth. It is a wonderful thing to see a beautiful woman's spirit break." He stood straight, stalking closer to me, his movements slow, lazy. "Tell me, Aenor. Do you know where to find my friend?"

I actually didn't, at least not with any precision. And that was damned lucky, because I had a feeling the moment he got what he wanted, I'd be dead.

"No."

"We'll see about that, Aenor. We'll see what you really know when I force it out of you." He took another step closer, and ghostly flames seemed to burn around him. His eyes grew brighter, gleaming like a riotous sunset.

I held his gaze, transfixed by him.

"You felt what I could do earlier," he purred. "I nearly forced you to cut your own wrist open. Now I need you to tell me what you actually know. Compelling you to answer some questions won't be difficult. You will bow to my control."

His magic boomed around me, pulsing through my blood, and I felt him claim my mind.

9

SALEM

I slowly crossed back to my desk, leaving her waiting, wondering what I'd do. Right now, my will had gripped her mind, and all she could do was stand there. Waiting.

And I was in no hurry to alleviate her sense of anticipation.

My cat, Aurora, rubbed against my legs, her loud purrs rumbling through the room.

I stole another glance at the morgen, her damp blue hair draped over her shoulders. Her beauty distracted me. And there was something about her scent I found disturbingly alluring. She smelled of sun-kissed sea air and wildflowers. And under that, something unique to her that drew me inexorably closer—something wild that I wanted to tame.

I pushed the errant thoughts from my mind.

From a drawer in my desk, I pulled out a bottle of 1858 cognac. I liked Aenor's eyes on me, knowing that I controlled her. I delighted in the sound of her heartbeat racing as she watched me. The scent of her fear warmed my blood.

The subjugation of a mortal foe tasted sweeter than brandy.

With an unhurried pace, I poured the cognac, then I let heat pulse from my palm to warm the glass. I took a sip, savoring the ancient, rich flavor—a rare bottle from before the best vineyards had been blighted.

In the cold ash of my soul, an ember burned. My heart rate seemed to be responding to Aenor's racing pulse.

Now *this* was a deeply unfamiliar feeling. Or more like a long-buried feeling, something left dormant in my mind for eons. It was like discovering a sensation lost to evolutionary history.

Was it the sense of victory making me excited?

I turned back to her, sniffing the cognac as I eyed her over the rim of the glass.

She stood, immobilized, waiting for my commands.

I stalked closer to her, watching her chest rise and fall faster at my approach. A little bit of panic began to take hold of her. Seawater dampened her top.

Once, long ago, I would have tortured the answers out of her, just like she said. I would have sunk my teeth into her perfect skin, delighted by her screams. Maybe I'd lost my appetite for such worldly pleasures, but evil deeds clung to a man like smoke. I'd never rid myself of the stench. Aenor could sense it on me, and it was making her panic.

I took another step around her, my gaze sliding over her damp clothes. I didn't delight in sadism these days. When I'd finished with her, I'd kill her fast. I should have done it long ago, but some insane impulse had stopped me from hurting her.

I let my magic beat from my body, invading her mind. Right now, she'd be hearing the drums of my enchantment magic pounding louder in her blood. I watched her back arch as my magic began to overtake her completely. She was glaring at me, pure hatred in her blue eyes. It seemed like a challenge I wanted to take on—*just try to tame me.*

I hadn't desired a woman in eons.

Except now.

My gaze swept down over her body, taking in her small waist and the perfect curves of her body. Her clothes clung to her. That was when a different sort of impulse ignited my mind.

Why torment her with pain when I could make her ache with sexual desire?

I wanted her bent over my desk, slick with desire. I wanted to see her writhing, moaning in erotic torment beneath me. I'd make her throb with a sexual ache so deep that she'd tell me anything I wanted. The fact that she despised me would only make her desire all the sweeter.

My breathing quickened as I started to speak in her mind. It was a god's voice, one she couldn't hear in normal words. She only knew that heat was swooping though her body. Already, I could hear her pulse racing. Her chest started rising and falling faster, pupils dilated.

My eyes flicked down to her perfect breasts, her nipples straining against the wet fabric. When her full lips parted, I imagined what it would feel like to kiss her, my tongue mingling with hers. Her body temperature rose, her blood pounding.

My mind danced with the image of Aenor crossing to my desk, unbuttoning her shorts. Her eyes would burn with lust, and she'd wonder why she couldn't control herself...

But with the look she was giving me, I could see right away that it wasn't *true* lust in her eyes. Her body might be warming with magical desire, but her hatred for me cut through it like a blade of ice.

And that look in her eyes snapped me out of my trance.

I gritted my teeth, mastering control of myself.

What the hells was getting into me? What was *that?*

I was turning into the Salem of old, the animal with a rapacious appetite for sex and violence. The one who lost focus at the slightest provocation. No—not really. Even in those days, I hadn't used this sort of magic to control women. There was no skill in that. Where was the glory in magical seduction?

I took a deep sip of my cognac, nearly draining it. Aenor had only been with me a few moments, and already I was losing control. The old beast was rising in me.

Don't lose sight of your destiny. The goddess Anat had given me a deadline, and I'd keep to it. After October thirty-first, when the darker half of the year began, it would all be over.

Once I'd mastered myself again, I began walking around Aenor, sweeping closer.

"Tell me exactly what you remember from that day. You trapped someone under the sea. Where was it?"

She closed her eyes, her breathing growing even faster. She *definitely* hated my invading her mind, but she was powerless to stop it. Her chest rose and fell fast, and my gaze dipped to it.

"It was midsummer." Her fingernails dug into her palms. "We had a big midsummer festival. You know how it goes. Apple groves, alcohol, dancing. People mating in the grass. Not me. I never did..." Her fingers dug deeper into her palms. "Well, there was one time—"

"I don't care who you did or did not mate with." Oddly, that was a lie. The idea of her locked in another man's embrace filled me with a strange sort of rage, but I wasn't going to examine that now. "Just tell me about when you slammed the ocean down on someone with immense magical power. That's what interests me."

"That night, I drank blueberry wine, and dandelion, then blackberry..."

"I get the idea. All varieties of wine. Move on to the part where you drowned someone?"

"The point is, my mom had given me all the wine. It was almost like she didn't want me to know entirely what was going on. She didn't want me asking too many questions, or knowing who we were trapping. She summoned me from the festival, and she had a boat waiting. She said someone was coming for Ys. Or... more than one person. She said our island would burn. It's just like now, with the Fomorians.

"And there was only one way to save the island," she went on. "And we had to act fast. We took the boat out to a smaller island, far out to sea—"

"What island?"

She shook her head, her jaw clenched like she was trying to keep her secrets. "I don't know. I remember rocks and grass? It was somewhere between Britain and Ireland. I'd been throwing up over the side of the boat for the whole journey. Maybe we were in the Celtic Sea or the English Channel. Anyway, we docked on a small island. I mean, very small. A mile, maybe. And off the coast, a glowing cage bobbed in the waves. Someone was in it. I couldn't see who."

"Go on."

Her nails dug deeper into her skin, drawing a little bit of blood. I wanted her to stop that, but I thought my magic was causing it.

Maybe she couldn't enchant me, but Aenor was already getting into my head.

10

SALEM

She opened her eyes, but they looked unfocused. "Then Mama grabbed me by the shoulders. She said, 'Aenor, I know you can't always handle all the power that the gods gave you.'" Aenor's accent had shifted, from American to a lilting Cornish. "'I know you feel like you're drowning in your magic sometimes. But the gods gave it to you for a reason, and you have a destiny. And this is it.'"

Her eyes focused again, sharpening on me. "Then my mother pointed at the driftwood cage. It was glowing in the sea. She told me if I didn't sink it, then Ys would be lost forever. I had to compel the ocean to cover it for good, so it could never rise again."

"And that was all it took for you."

She wiped a shaking hand across her mouth, like she was trying to stop herself from speaking. I saw a glimpse of the streak of blood on her palm, and my throat tightened.

"No. Like I said, I did a spell for myself. Back when I had my magic, I could do little spells to see the future. Or the possibilities of the future. I called them *what if* spells. I wanted to see what would happen if we let this fae do what he wanted. And what I found was pure destruction."

"Is that so?" *How very wrong you are.*

"He was going to destroy Ys first, then the world beyond. Do you know what I saw?" Her voice had gone low, intense. "I saw seas boiling and drying up. I saw the future—a column of rock crushing my own skull, blood leaking over the hot marble. And all the little children of Ys turned to dust and blew away on the wind. Then the destruction moved on to the rest of the world, leaving a trail of death."

She took a deep, shaking breath. She really believed this.

"So I did what they asked," she went on. "We were the protectors of the sea, it was our job to keep it safe. Just like it's my job to stop the Fomorians now. It's the same thing, and somehow, it's all connected to you."

"And you've based this on your *what if* spell."

"It's never been wrong. I'd do one now, but you haven't given me my power back. So yes, I used my power over the sea to drag your friend to the bottom of the ocean. I buried that cage, because I had to. And it's still there."

I felt a wild impulse to believe her, against my better judgment. And yet I knew the woman she'd drowned—a goddess who had no desire to burn anything. Coldness slid through my veins as I thought of her alone under the sea. If I'd known she was still alive down there, I'd have come for her sooner.

"What did she say when you drowned her?" I asked.

Aenor now looked completely alert. "*She?* She didn't say a thing when I pulled her under the waves. I didn't know she was female. All my mother's enemies were men." Her expression was resolute. "But I know what I saw with my *what if* spell. And if you unleash her on the world, she'll burn it."

My lip curled. "I really don't care what happens to this wretched world. But just so you know, you were wrong. You drowned someone with great power, but she had no desire to burn the world down. That's more my thing."

I was feeling something again, but it wasn't sweet revenge. I felt a strange twist in my chest when I watched Aenor digging her nails into her palms again.

"So how do I find her?" My voice chilled the room. "If you don't know where she is? Will your magic get us to her?"

Her jaw tightened as she fought my control over her. Each one of her muscles went rigid, her cheeks flushing. She was using every bit of restraint she could muster. Truthfully, she was holding out longer than I'd imagined, but she couldn't resist forever.

"Merrow." It was as if the word had been wrenched out of her.

Something flashed in her eyes, but I wasn't sure what it was. Rage, perhaps.

"The Merrow will know where to find her," she said through gritted teeth. "He's probably somewhere near the British Isles. He never strays far. But I can't be more precise than that until I have my magic back. I remember what his magic sounds like under the sea. Once I have my power, I'll be able to track him, even if he's far away. I can take you to him."

I went still. "And why can't you just track her directly, once you have your power? Why must we find this Merrow first?"

Her body went rigid, jaw tensing. "I don't know what her magic sounds like. I won't be able to pick it out from the other noise in the sea. The Merrow's I remember. I know the sound of his magic, and I can find it in the sea."

"How did the Merrow trap her?"

She was shooting me a look of death. "He made a soul cage and trapped the fae. It tethered her body and soul into a cage of driftwood. She's still alive in the soul cage, but can't escape. The charmed driftwood pulled her magic from her body."

Wrath slid through my bones.

As soon as Aenor helped me find who I was looking for, I should complete the task I'd failed at years ago. She deserved death, my blade through her neck.

Once I achieved my destiny, nothing else mattered. I wouldn't let her beauty pull me off my task.

I released my control on Aenor's mind, and her muscles started to relax. My chest unclenched a little as she calmed down.

Her chest rose and fell fast, and she pushed her wet hair out of her face. "Who is she? The woman in the cage?"

I sipped my brandy. "Perhaps you should have asked this question before you drowned her."

"She's obviously important to you."

I swirled the brandy in my glass. "I think the time for your questions about her has passed."

She took a step closer. I read hunger in her large blue eyes. "Okay. So when will I be getting my magic back?" She craved her magic more than anything. "And how?"

"You'll get it from me, soon. I have the power to steal magic, at least for a time. I can hold it in my body and transfer it between people. I've stored your power in an urn."

"An urn?" she repeated. "Like what you'd keep human ashes in?"

I raised an eyebrow. Was she mad? "I would not keep human ashes in an urn. In any case, I'll pull the magic back into my own body, then I'll reflect it back into you. I can channel it slowly, so you're not overwhelmed. You can use me and the earth to ground the magic."

For the first time, I saw Aenor smile unguardedly, if only for a moment. Beautiful.

Then the guarded look overtook her features once more, and the light was gone from the room. "Let's do it now."

The corner of my lip twitched. I *did* like making her wait for things she craved. "Tell me, Aenor. You have lived for a hundred and sixty years. Am I right in thinking you never took a long-term lover before Lyr?"

She crossed her arms. "You really don't have anything better to worry about than my dating history?"

"I just wonder what it was about him that changed your mind after so many years."

She pressed her hand to her chest. "Why, Devil Himself, are you jealous? You do flatter me."

The insane thing was—yes. I was jealous. "Do you know what I think it is? Lyr travels in and out of the death worlds. He rules the realm of the dead. And that's what you crave, isn't it? Oblivion. Death. Sweet release from this world that you've tired of, now that you can't feel any more. Your magic is gone, and so is your feeling of living. And now you need reprieve from those terrible thoughts and memories that play in your mind. That's what drew you to Lyr. Oblivion."

Aenor's satisfied smile faltered, and she looked like someone had slapped her across the face. I'd hit the mark exactly.

Then she composed herself and beamed again. "I think you might be projecting just a bit. That's what humans say when they want to tell you that you're talking about yourself and don't realize it. You crave death, don't you? Because nearly the entirety of living history hates you down to your bones. What's the point of living if nobody loves you? I don't have a lot, but I've always had a friend or two."

Hollowness yawned in my chest, and I fell silent.

Hells, perhaps we had more in common than I'd liked to admit. Maybe we both craved oblivion.

I brushed my gaze down her body again, taking in her wet clothes. "You can get ready before our journey in one of the guest rooms, if you like. Then meet me in the garden. You'll get your power back, and we'll head to the British Isles."

Soon, I'd fulfill my destiny. I'd find the soul cage; I'd kill Aenor. I'd do this all before October thirty-first.

Then true glory would be mine once more.

11

AENOR

I stood in Salem's shower, pale stone walls around me. So far, everything was working out as I'd hoped. I'd get my magic back; we'd find the Merrow. I'd get the sea glass.

And Salem thought it was all his idea.

But even with the Merrow's help, I wasn't under the illusion that it would be easy to kill Salem. He was dangerous as hell. In the dark magic that slid around him, I felt torment. It was like a perpetual warning to anyone who came near him that he might burn you to death. He might flash you a seductive smile, then rip your soul from your body.

Now, at last, I knew why Salem had destroyed Ys. It was punishment for drowning this woman who wanted to burn the world down. Ironic, I guess, that in trying to keep Ys safe, we'd brought on its demise. Still, at least the people had survived. No one turned to hot dust in the wind.

I let the water stream over my face.

What I wanted to do was another *what if* spell. I needed my magic back for that. Then I needed to be alone.

What if I failed to stop Salem? I had a feeling it would look as fiery and destructive as the first time.

I'd turned the water up so hot that it turned my skin pink. I grabbed the soap, which smelled faintly of lemons, and lathered myself up, washing off the dried sea salt. Steam billowed around me.

Who was this woman I'd drowned?

Salem was desperate to get her back. He didn't seem like the type of person who would care about anyone but himself, so I had to wonder.

Was she his mate, perhaps?

I turned off the shower, and water streamed down my body as I stepped out. Fragrant air skimmed in through the open window onto my bare skin.

As I toweled off my hair, I stared down across the wide courtyard. Salem lived in what I'd call a palace. Where I stood now, I was two stories above the garden. Beneath me, fig and apple trees lined a dirt path.

Was it just me, or did the worst people have the best lives?

I watched as Salem crossed out into his garden, bathed in the moonlight. He moved smoothly in the darkness, his cat hurrying after him on the garden path. I could see my magic glowing around his body.

Euphoria rose in my chest at the thought of how my magic would feel reunited with my body.

With a sense of building excitement, I crossed naked out of the bathroom into a bedroom. The guest room looked ancient—rough stone walls, a metal chandelier hanging from the ceiling. Statues stood in arched alcoves—mostly depicting women in obscene positions, but the stonework was masterful.

Someone had laid out a clean set of clothes on the silky

duvet—a simple black miniskirt and a button-down shirt. I dressed myself, singing Elvis's "*Suspicious Minds*" to myself quietly as I did.

I'd lost my shoes in the swim, but someone had left another pair by the bed—exactly my size. I slid into them. Cleaned and fully dressed, I crossed out of the bedroom.

I rushed down the stairs. But on the landing, I paused. A painting hung on the wall, flanked by torches. Except a silk cloth covered the frame.

A sharp pull of curiosity compelled me to peer under the cloth, holding my breath. Under it, I found an image in oils of a beautiful woman. An eight-pointed star gleamed in her forehead, and wings swept down her back. Silver hair tumbled over a pale gold gown. Lavender and peach light lit up a sky behind her. My breath caught in my throat.

This was her, I was certain. This was the woman in the driftwood soul cage.

For a moment, confronted with her face, I felt something like guilt.

Then my jaw tightened. Like I'd said to Salem, I did what I had to do to protect the seas.

I trusted my vision, even if Salem didn't.

I covered the image again and rushed down the rest of the stairs. At the bottom, a set of glass doors opened to the garden.

I pulled open the doors. Fig and apple trees grew on either side of a path, and grapevines clung to the outer stone walls. Mushrooms circled some of the tree trunks, and blood-red flowers carpeted the floor. This whole place was beautiful.

As my eyes adjusted to the dark, I caught sight of Salem down the path, my blue-green magic shimmering around his muscled body.

The alluring scent of the garden washed over me. Salem leaned back against a tree, sipping his wine. His eyes burned with fiery hues as he watched me. The breeze ruffled his hair a little. He really looked like he had not a care in the world. Strange that he should be so at ease when the smoky magic spooling off him made my chest ache with fear.

And then there was the music of his magic.

For some creatures, the sound of their magic was as melodious and sweet as cherubs playing harps.

In Salem's case? It sounded like primal drums echoing off cave walls. And underneath the drums, distant screams. *That* was his magic.

Everything about him unsettled me, and his heart-breaking beauty only enhanced the effect. No wonder the Lucifer stories he'd inspired were ones of temptation and despair, of seduced women and lost souls.

As I drew closer, I realized I could smell something else on him—my sea magic. The air tasted of salt, and I felt a charge of watery magic skimming my skin.

As I moved closer, the magnetic pull between us felt overwhelming. Something tugged me to him, and I closed the distance until I was standing only inches from him. I just wanted to bask in the feel of my magic, and it tingled over my skin.

Already, the moonlight seemed a little brighter, silvery on his dark hair.

He lowered his wineglass, his gaze meeting mine for a long time. He towered over me, and I realized his face was a perfect study of contrasts—fiery eyes and dark lashes, masculine jaw and sensual lips.

But the real question was—how the hells could he look so relaxed while channeling magic that powerful? My own magic made me half insane.

"I'm ready for my magic," I said.

Without a word, he reached for my waist. As soon as he made contact with me, his hand channeled electrifying magic into my body. A rush of power coiled into my body from his, and I felt my back arch. Power swept into my body from the points of his fingers, from his palm—a rushing charge that flooded me from that one point of contact and vibrated through my belly. It rolled into my thighs, my legs, my chest and arms, and I gasped.

As my body filled with magic, my mind blazed with images of an ocean's surface, pierced with golden rays of light—a cathedral of life.

Life. The ocean was life, and its power was washing into me. Already, I could feel my body growing stronger. I possessed the strength of a fae goddess.

My senses started to heighten, and I could hear the blackbirds' song around me. Not just their song but their *heartbeats,* their breaths. I could hear Salem's heart, too, pounding loud as a drum. And his sensual magic was like tongues licking over my skin. He smelled like sin…

Oh *gods,* I could hear the plants growing slowly around me. The rich scent of the soil curled around me, and with it, figs and apples, their smell heavy with sweet sensuality.

A warm breeze skimmed my skin like a caress. *Yes.*

I opened my eyes, staring up at the starry sky. The stars were no longer distant points. They pulsed above me, living and dying creatures—some of them red with old age, some mere clouds of beaming dust. Life and beauty everywhere around me.

Venus blazed blue in the sky, so stunning I could hardly breathe. The cold, dusky beauty of its light was like a million pieces of glass shattering in my heart. It was the beauty of Salem…

Humans once called that the evening star—a god of twilight, like Salem himself. I turned to look into his eyes and found the same silver-blue as the evening star above us. His face was masculine perfection, carved by the gods. Would he look at me that way when I shoved the sea glass into his heart?

There was no one else but us, so close our breath mingled... His powerful energy was like a force of nature around me.

It took me a moment to realize that I'd pressed myself against his body, hips crushed against his. In my delirium, I'd draped one of my arms around his neck. He smelled of smoke and pomegranates, and a faint light gleamed on his forehead.

His heart beat against me, and his eyes burned brightly. He wrapped an arm around me, and I leaned into its power. He moved one of his fingertips over my hipbone, the touch light. Such a subtle touch, but deeply sexual. I was so trans-fixed that I couldn't remember how to pull away from him.

One corner of his lip curled in a wicked smile. "I see we're getting to know each other better." His voice skimmed over my skin, velvet soft. "Though I imagine you have some half-baked plan to kill me."

Slowly, I pulled myself away from him, my limbs humming. I wanted to eat everything in the garden. I reached up to pull an apple from the tree above him and bit into it. Its sweet tang exploded on my tongue.

"The ocean is the source of all life," I said, then realized my mouth was full of apple. I swallowed. "And I'm alive again. And I'm going to keep it safe."

"Well, good luck with that, Aenor. But for now, we're going home. Back to the British Isles."

Waves of magic crashed through my blood. I felt like I

could destroy worlds. Gods, I wasn't sure if I wanted to kiss someone or rip a person's heart out. Maybe both?

"Home." I'd be heading back toward the cold Atlantic waters where I was born.

A star beneath the sea... Driftwood to keep her trapped...

I touched my temples, struggling to form coherent thoughts. My old magic would take some getting used to.

Salem prowled closer, eyes locked on me. "Use the feel of the earth beneath you to ground your magic. Channel it so it moves in and out through your feet."

I did as he asked, envisioning the magic like flowing water, moving up and down my legs. It helped me settle the surge of power a little, though it still trembled though my body.

"Once we get to the sea," he said, "I'll make sure you're in control. I can't have you drowning all of Europe while we're trying to find the driftwood cage. It's not on my agenda."

Truly, I'd never fully mastered sea magic. I'd experimented, though. I could make steam from my fingertips. I could lure the sea to me like a gravitational force, and command the waves to drown Europe, like Salem had suggested. I could form blades and weapons of ice from my hands. I could suck all the water from a person's body, leaving them a desiccated husk that could blow away in the wind.

I stared at Salem, wondering if I should just *try* doing that to him. I cocked my head, letting the sea magic crackle over my body.

But as soon as I lifted my hand, he began to glow with sunset colors. He was protecting himself against my magic. Or maybe he was just naturally immune to it.

Whatever the case, it wasn't working.

"Well, that must be disappointing." A cruel smile ghosted over his lips.

I shrugged. "I was just testing it out."

"You can't kill me, Aenor. Only one person can kill me, and it's not you."

Hmmm. Not what the Winter Witch said, but I wasn't about to out myself.

Another wave of power crashed through me, and my teeth chattered at its force. "Fine. How are we getting to the British Isles?"

"Follow me." He brushed past me, his magic mingling with mine.

As I walked behind him, my thoughts swarmed, beauty and terror intermingling. I felt like the wind was singing to me.

I was, perhaps, tripping out. But godsdamn, it felt good to trip out on my magic.

I sighed, and an image blazed in my mind—sea glass carving out Salem's heart.

But the vision didn't feel as victorious as I'd imagined. It felt wrong.

All the magic coursing through my veins abhorred death. I wanted *life* now.

Still, when the time came, I would do what I needed to do. I'd end his life for good.

12

SALEM

I led Aenor into the stone tunnel below ground. When she turned to look at me, I saw that her pupils had gone wide and dark, her cheeks rosy. She looked so *alive* that it almost made my pulse race.

Holding her magic in my body had felt like an illicit thrill. I was merely a channeler of her magic—a vessel—so I couldn't wield it like she could. But I still felt it charge my veins. There was an intimacy to it.

It was a magic more intense than anything I'd experienced. Now, it ran through the veins of the beautiful body of the woman before me. A miniskirt, heels, and magic as powerful as a thousand suns.

I nearly forgot Ossian was with us, until one of his birds circled around my head. He bit into an apple, slouching as he walked.

Ossian's sea magic wasn't nearly as impressive as Aenor's, but at least he was fully in control of it. Who knew what she would do? She was a complete wild card, and she seemed half delirious.

Why did she interest me so much? Maybe it was because

her entire demeanor had changed. Now that her body glowed with sea magic, her movements were languid. Sensual, almost. My gaze lingered on her bare legs.

If I were the man I used to be, I'd think of pulling her into a shadowy offshoot of this tunnel. I'd imagine myself sliding my hand up her thigh, kissing her deeply. The Salem of years ago would think of her naked, splayed out before him.

But those thoughts belonged to the person I *used* to be. Back when humans drew on cave walls. That part of my soul was now as lifeless as the rocky walls around us. Ever since I'd been banished from *Mag Mell* tens of thousands of years ago.

I watched as she trailed her fingertips along the wall, humming quietly to herself. Her hips swayed, like she was *trying* to entice me.

I breathed in the air, heavy with moss and dirt. A thousand years ago, a cabal of bloodthirsty crusaders had created this enchanted tunnel—a secret passage that magically shortened the distance between England and Jerusalem. Quite convenient for me, really.

Aenor's footfalls echoed off the cave walls.

Silver moonlight filtered in through the end of the tunnel, and the salty air floated in on the breeze.

The tunnel was leading us to Brighton, on the south coast of England. There, the Atlantic waters flowed into the English Channel.

Aenor turned to me, her wide blue eyes bright in the darkness. "Tell me something, Mr. Lucifer. How did you end up all the way in Jerusalem? You're from the British Isles. All fae come from the British Isles originally."

"I wandered."

Her eyes narrowed. "And you're really *the* Lucifer? The

one that humans talk about? The light-bringer? The root of all evil?" Her tone was light, like it was all a joke to her. "The vilest creature in the history of the world?"

I stared at her, wishing I'd brought more brandy. "I'm not a chronicler of human culture. You'd have to ask one of them."

"Were you in some kind of hell?"

You naive little thing. You really have no idea. "You could say that."

She turned away from me, no longer interested in her line of questioning.

"I can feel the ocean calling to me," she said quietly to herself, but I picked up the sound. Hope lit up her voice, and a new sensation stirred in my heart.

13

AENOR

My sea magic surged through my veins.

I bit my lip, trying to think clearly as the tunnel opened up into a wooden arcade hall. Dark in the dead of night, pinball machines and video games crowded the Victorian building. When I turned, I saw that the tunnel opening had disappeared behind us.

We were so close to the sea now that I could taste it...

This would be an amazing time to enchant Salem with my morgen powers, except that he was impervious to them now.

I'd have to use subtler methods. Except it was hard to be subtle when you were drowning in sensations.

Even in the darkness, the moonlight streaming through the windows seemed too bright, and our quiet footfalls boomed in my ears. I was quickly remembering how it felt to be overwhelmed by magic—and why I used to drink so much to quiet the world down.

Even inside the arcade hall, the scent of the sea hit me hard, seaweed and brine curling around me. I wanted to plunge into the ocean's cool depths. I craved its darkness, the quiet under the water.

I flashed Salem a dark smile, thrilled at how my body felt—like the sea was crashing through my muscles.

Salem pushed through a door onto a wooden pier, and at that point, I knew just where we were. *Brighton.*

Along with the brine, I caught the sugary scent of donuts in the air. I turned, my body wild.

Below the pier, waves crashed against the pebbled shore. The sound was like my own heartbeat.

As I walked along the pier, I kicked off my heels, walking over the boards barefoot. The sea spray dampened my face. Screw high heels. Why did I wear those things? I didn't need to be taller.

Ossian lifted his arms in the air. He still wasn't wearing a shirt. What was it with fae males and not wearing shirts?

"We're home!" he shouted at the sea.

I glanced at the ocean to the left of the pier, and the force of it hit me like a fist. All that power, all that life, glittering bright under the moonlight. I felt in tune with the distant sea turtles, sharks, tiny mollusks in shells drifting through the shadowy quiet... ice floes in the north... For a moment, dizziness whirled in my mind, and I had to steady myself, gripping the wooden railing. I took a deep breath, pulse racing.

It's too much... I was going to lose my damn mind.

I closed my eyes, trying to ground myself by thinking of the steadiness of the wood beneath my feet. Slowly, I got some control again.

But what I really wanted was something familiar. Some*one* familiar. A friend.

I imagined myself sitting at home in the ol' dirt hole

with Gina, eating a cheap pizza. She'd demand pineapples on it, the maniac.

Shit... Gina. I hadn't thought about it until now, but Lyr was the one who'd arranged for her to stay at the Savoy. What if—what if he used her as leverage to get to me?

I bit my lip. He wouldn't do that, would he? I didn't think he would...

Suddenly, I had a desperate urge to talk to her.

"Why do you look like you're about to lose your lunch, Aenor of Meriadoc?" asked Salem.

I turned to Ossian. "Do you have a mobile phone?"

He stared at me. "You want to use a mobile phone now?"

"I just need to call someone. One minute, tops. Just, like, a check-in."

"Who and why?" he asked.

For crying out loud, I hated having to explain myself to him. "A human friend, and I just want to say hi and see how she is. And make sure she's okay."

Salem took a step closer, eyes burning with curiosity. Something cold and dangerous crackled up my spine.

Then he nodded at Ossian, who pulled out his cell phone.

I brought up the internet to search for the Savoy Hotel, then dialed the number. Energy coursed wildly through my veins, and I bounced from foot to foot as I asked to be connected to Gina's room.

As the phone rang, we started walking again, heading for the foot of the pier. My heart hammered as I waited for her to answer.

After a few moments, she picked up. "Yeah?"

"Gina. I can't talk long. I just wanted to tell you that I got my magic back." I held my hand over the phone, whispering. "All of it. I'm a sea goddess now. I can merge with ocean life. The moon is so bright, Gina. *The sea is life.*"

A long pause hung in the air. "Are you high?"

"High on magic," I whispered.

"Okay, you need to settle down. Get a snack."

"But the thing is—" I shot a sharp look at Salem and Ossian, who were watching me, and stepped away from them. I whispered, "Look, I don't want to go into it right now, but do you have a friend you can stay with instead of staying in the Savoy?"

"Seriously?"

"Seriously."

"I might, yeah. Gemma. But now? I'm watching a TV show about women who are competing to get funding for plastic surgery. They have to do these dance routines to win. One of them, this woman from Essex named Jenna, just did a Pennywise-themed striptease. You know, like the scary clown from the movie *It*?"

I blinked. "That's... I don't know what to say to that. Can you get to your friend's house? And don't speak to any knights."

"Yeah. Fine. I'm on it."

I took a deep breath. "I gotta go."

I turned off the phone and handed it back to Ossian. We'd arrived on the slick stones that filled Brighton's shoreline. The rocks felt smooth and perfect beneath my feet.

I stepped closer to the waves, until the cold Atlantic water lapped over my toes. This was my domain. Some of the wildness arcing through me began to simmer down, and I focused on the feel of my feet on the stones.

"What happens next?" I asked.

Salem's eyes burned bright in the darkness. "You wade

into the water, and you tell me how to get to the Merrow. Without causing any tsunamis."

"And what are you going to do if I do cause a tsunami?"

He nodded at Ossian. "He's here to help control the waves if you do."

Ossian's birds fluttered around his head. He blew out a puff of smoke, then dropped his joint on the wet rocks. "You can count on me."

The rocks seemed to rumble rhythmically beneath my feet. *Boom. Boom. Boom.*

But this wasn't Salem's magic.

"Hang on," I said. "I hear something."

Ossian turned, his attention caught by something in the distance. "Do you see that?"

Salem's body tensed.

I narrowed my eyes, trying to pick out what they were seeing. Just tiny pinpricks in the distance. But their magic pounded over the rocks.

Salem turned to me, eyes cold and blue as dusk. "Did you call these sea creatures forth?"

I blinked. "Me? No. I wish I had, though. Brilliant idea."

Salem took a step closer, towering over me as his eyes bored into mine. His magic had a sensual feel on my skin, like a forbidden touch. "How convenient for you, that group of armed sea fae are heading for us right now. Perhaps that phone call had something to do with it?"

He pulled his sword from its sheath, and flames flickered over the naked blade.

I felt as if ice were sliding down from my shoulders to my wrists, and my fingers tightened into fists. I stared down the beach at the sea fae running for us.

Like Salem, they had swords, though theirs weren't on fire.

"I didn't call them," I said. "And I don't think they're coming to help me."

Instinctively, magic snaked down my arm, until a sword of ice formed in my palm. It glinted in the moonlight.

"Prove it, then," Salem said. "Kill them."

A shiver rippled up my spine, mingling with the rush of magic.

The sea fae's bodies glowed as they moved closer, air slick and wet around us. I counted six of them.

To my left, the ocean receded, but it wasn't me controlling it now. Ossian was using his magic to summon a wave that would slam into our attackers. They were nearly upon us.

One of them was heading right for me, his scaled skin glistening in the moonlight. His long green hair streamed behind him, and his teeth were sharp points. Just a few feet away from me, he raised his sword over his head, ready to strike my head from my body.

Definitely not a rescue mission.

Instinct took over, and I lunged forward, swinging my sword to meet the attacker's. *I am a queen of the sea.*

My blade went through his neck, swift as a storm wind. The creature's head rolled into the sea.

A loud rumbling heralded the arrival of a monstrous ocean wave. As it curved over us, droplets of spray sparked into the air like magic then disappeared in the air. Then the waved slammed down.

I absorbed its power, thrilling at the feel of it.

As the wave receded, I managed to hold my ground. The ocean had eaten up some of our attackers.

But from the darkness, more sea fae charged for us, hair streaming behind.

Salem's power boomed over the horizon, and I stole a

glance at him—*up* at him. Feathered wings had grown from his back, and dark horns had grown from his shoulder blades, piercing the fabric of his expensive suit. From above, he swooped closer to the sea fae. He dove for the attackers like a vengeful god, blade moving in a blur of holy fire.

His sword arced through the air, slicing bodies in two. Severed halves of sea fae slid into the waves with a sickening splash.

I refocused on the ground, getting ready for the next line of attackers to make it past Salem.

I brought my sword down into a fae before me, carving through his neck. But another had slipped behind me, clawed fingers digging into my throat.

I unleashed a burst of magic and wriggled free from his grasp. But the sea fae were surrounding me, grabbing my limbs and my throat. One of them pressed into me.

His eyes opened wide, murky as the sea.

I let icy claws grow from my fingertips, then plunged them into his stomach. "Who sent you?" I asked.

"The Merrow..." he croaked.

Another powerful ocean wave slammed down on us, and it felt like home. The sea ripped my attackers from me, and I stood tall.

When the wave receded, I found that it had sucked some of the sea fae into its churn.

But they were rising again. Sea magic surged within me, sliding down my bones like ice floes. Whirling, I threw myself into the battle. I moved fast as a sea gale, ripping attackers to shreds with my claws of ice. From the corner of my eye, I saw Salem fighting them too, severing bodies with his sword.

Death pounded in my blood like a sacrificial drum.

The Merrow...

How had the Merrow already figured out we were coming for him? I needed to get a message to him. I needed him to know I was on his side.

An attacker ran for me. Shards of ice exploded from my fingertips, landing with precision in one of the Merrow's men. I closed my eyes, overcome by the wild rush of magic pounding through my body.

I can kill them all.

I threw back my arms, and sea magic burst from my ribs. Pure, euphoric ecstasy. I opened my eyes, surveying the glacial world around me. Ice encased everything...

I am a goddess of the cold sea...

I stared at a world of ice and raised my hands above my head.

All will fall before me. All will sacrifice to the sea goddess if they want to live.

With a dark thrill, I was calling the cold sea to me.

Salem was speaking to me, but I tuned out his silken voice.

I will bathe the world in my power.

An icy wave slammed down on us, a thousand tons of water and ice. I stood tall, absorbing the force of it. Its energy slammed into my own, and I felt life rushing around me. An orchestra of the ocean's music boomed.

As the wave receded, I looked around at my work.

The other sea fae lay dead on the rocky beach, bodies frozen in contorted positions.

I rule the icy Atlantic. My frozen gaze slid over to the city of Brighton. I had the power to drown it all...

I could drown the whole world.

14

AENOR

A hot hand on my waist pulled me from my apocalyptic visions, and warmth spread over my skin from the point of contact. The scent of pomegranates woke me from my delirium, and the heat of Salem's body beamed around me like sun rays. Strange that it felt so comforting, like I was melting into him.

I sighed as I felt some of my magic slip out of my body, into his hand. A relief. I'd been so desperate for my power, but it was too much.

I thought I heard him make a low, quiet noise in his throat as I pressed back into him...

"Don't take it all," I said.

"I wouldn't dream of it." His breath was soft against my ear.

After that great rush of power, my legs were shaking.

Slowly, Salem pulled his hand from me. "I left you with most of it."

At least I could think clearly again. Trembling, I stepped away and turned to face him. "I'm not used to it anymore."

His eyes glinted. "I did get that impression when you said you were going to drown the whole world."

"I didn't realize I'd said that out loud." My mind sparked with that image of the bodies floating in a world of icy water. "I shouldn't have it all back."

Salem flashed a smile and sheathed his sword. "But the destruction you could wreak would be breathtaking."

"Maybe. But I have better things to do than destroy the world." *Hula-hooping, Elvis records... cutting your heart out with sea glass.* All kinds of fun stuff. "What did you do with my magic?"

Salem held up a hand, and a ring shone on one of his fingers. Blue-green magic glittered around it. "It's here if we need it."

"Probably best if I don't," I muttered. I surveyed the icy beach around us.

Ossian stood hugging himself, teeth chattering. Frost whitened his eyebrows.

"Bit much, Aenor," he grumbled.

Salem crossed to one of the frozen fae and knelt down. He was examining the soldier's forearm, encased in ice. As I moved closer to peer over his shoulder, I could see what he was looking at. It was a tattoo beneath the ice—a trident encircled by a snake eating its tail.

"Do you happen to know what this symbol is?" asked Salem. "Looks like a sea fae thing."

I did. It was the Merrow's symbol. "The Merrow is trying to stop you from getting what you want. He knows you're on the right track."

Salem shot me a sharp look. "And you have no idea how they knew to come for us?"

"He's a powerful sorcerer. I'm sure he can see us coming, whether or not someone tipped him off."

The unfortunate thing was that perhaps the Merrow would try to murder us throughout our entire journey. How could I get a message to him?

"How convenient for you that he threw this obstacle in my path." Salem's voice was dark as midnight.

I gestured at the bodies. "How is it convenient? I just killed them all. I'm getting nothing out of this situation except that I just pissed off a powerful sorcerer."

"Perhaps." He glanced at the ocean, at the raging waves slowly dying down, then slid his hands into his pockets. "Go on, then. Tell me where to find the Merrow."

I started to wander into the icy waves. In the ocean, my limbs relaxed, leaving behind a gentle buzz. The sea felt soothing against my tired legs, and it enveloped me as I plunged into it.

As I sank under the waves, home once more, the music of the ocean sang around me. And I just had to home in on the sound of the Merrow.

Problem was that there was so much of it—a swelling orchestra of sounds—that it was nearly impossible to find the right song. Magical creatures filled the sea—mermaids, selkies, morgens like me. Their music vibrated all around me.

I remembered what the Merrow's song sounded like, but his harmony was lost in the din.

Still, I had a way to home in on one particular person. I just needed a small sacrifice to the god of the sea.

Gods loved sacrifices.

I scrambled around on the seafloor until I found a sharp bit of seashell. I snatched it off the stones, then swam deeper into the cold ocean. Rays of moonlight streamed through the waves.

Basically, the gods were emotionally needy jerks who

craved proof of devotion in the form of dead goats or precious jewels or virgins tossed into volcanos. They fed off drama and misery.

And yes, I could ask them to take me directly to this soul cage, but that wasn't my true destination.

As it happened, I was fresh out of goats and virgins. But I could offer my own blood.

I took the shard of seashell and reached down to my thigh. I cut into it, wincing a little as the seashell sliced my skin. My blood pooled and clouded in the dark water.

I started to hum a melody—the song of the Merrow, stored in my brain after all these years.

God of the sea, help me hear this music I seek.

I hummed louder, picturing him as vividly as I could— his old, stooped form, a slouching red hat, his gnarled wooden staff.

I stared as my blood snaked through the water, and the music around me dulled to quiet.

At last, only one song remained—a multi-tonal chant. The Merrow's song threaded through the water.

I couldn't pinpoint *exactly* where he was, but I had a vague idea. Right now, we were on the southern coast of England, and the sounds were coming from the... north-west, I thought. Up along the west coast, maybe out in the Irish Sea? I was nearly positive.

I turned, swimming back to the shoreline. I should have felt ecstatic that I'd made progress. Get magic, find Merrow. Instead, I felt a dim sense of dread.

As I stepped from the ocean, I stared at the solitary figure on the shoreline. Ossian had left, and Salem stood alone. His dark wings, so like an angel's, cascaded behind him.

The sight of a winged fae was a rare thing indeed. His

dark feathers faded to a dusky violet at the tips, and streaks of fiery gold shot through them. Lonely and dramatic, the colors of twilight.

"Well?" he asked.

"Northwest. The closer we get, the easier it will be for me to tune in to the sound of his magic. I don't suppose you can swim with those wings."

"Swimming for days is not among my many talents. And that's where you come in. I've just returned your immense power to you. What do you need to do to get us to the right place? Part the seas?"

"*Part the seas?* That would be disastrous for the sea life on the ocean floor. I mean, the coral alone—"

"What gave you the impression I would give a fuck about coral?" he asked.

"It wouldn't get us to him anyway. I need to hear the music in the ocean. I have another way."

"Wait." His icy gaze slid to my thigh where I'd cut myself. Then his eyes flashed with pale blue. His entire body tensed. "Why are you bleeding?"

"A little sacrifice to the sea god. It's fine."

"Sacrifice..." He shifted over to me, a blur of darkness.

In the next moment, one of his hands was around my waist, and the other was coiled around my thigh, pulling it up. Healing magic slid over my leg, around my skin, and Salem stared at it as the wound closed up. Heat radiated from his body, and my pulse sped up.

"What are you doing?" I said. "It was a small cut."

"No sacrifices." His warm magic slowly caressed my skin.

I stared at him, dumbfounded. "That's how the gods grant you things." I enunciated it slowly, like I was talking to a child. "It's how a lot of magic works."

"No sacrifices," he said again, fire flashing in his eyes.

For a man so sophisticated on the outside, there was something distinctly bestial about him. "The gods don't need you to prove your love. If you need more magic, I'll give it to you."

When my leg had healed, I pulled myself out of his grip. "Are you jealous of the worship the gods inspire?"

The warmth of his body contrasted sharply with the pure ice in his eyes. "You said you had another way to get us to the Merrow. Why don't you show me now?"

I waded back into the sea, breathing in the briny air, and lifted my arms. Here, with the sea lapping at my legs, I could almost hear the forlorn bells of Ys. They'd tolled at high tide and low.

Magic raced through my body, and the sea sparkled before me with phosphorescence to rival the stars. I took another step deeper into the waves and swirled my hand before me, until the waters began to froth and heave.

Slowly, from the sea foam, a boat began to emerge, a gleaming mist billowing around it.

Wind filled a single square sail—shades of blue and gold. In the center of the sail, the symbol of the Meriadoc family was emblazoned—a horse, rising from a churning sea. Seashells dotted the side of the boat, arranged in curling forms. I gripped the side of the hull.

Then I turned to find Salem staring at me, a curious expression on his face.

I beckoned him to the boat. "Come on. Our ride is here."

Without a word, he followed me to the sailboat and climbed inside. Seats lined the sides of the boat, and I sat in the prow. It would sail itself, with my mind guiding it.

When I looked up again at Salem, his wings had disappeared. He leaned back against the side of the boat, a smile on his lips, and pulled a flask from his pocket. He unscrewed it and took a sip. His eyes twinkled in the darkness. "And here we go. Let's fix what you did all those years ago."

Yes, let's do that.

Let's fix the mistake I made when I failed to drown you years ago along with your friend.

15

SALEM

We drifted over the ocean waves, sea spray cooling my skin. As Aenor guided us expertly over the sea, I felt the winds rising faster around us. An electrical charge hung in the air. Aenor trailed her fingertips in the water over the side of the boat, her eyes on the skies. Avoiding me, probably.

Aenor shifted on the seat. She seemed a restless spirit, always moving, eyes always scanning.

Above us, dark clouds slowly slid over the moon and stars. The ocean waves grew choppier as we sailed, spray washing over us.

In the distance, I heard the sound of crows cawing wildly. Hundreds of them, it sounded like.

And that would be the Isle of Crows. Aptly named.

I glanced down at Aenor's feet. Barefoot in the boat, one foot tapping. She'd discarded her shoes somewhere. Catching sight of me looking at her, she sat up straight. Her gaze flicked to the ring at my finger, glowing with her magic. It was strangely intoxicating—the smell of it, the feel of it sliding over my skin. A perverse part of me wanted to see her wield all of her magic with complete abandon.

I held up my hand with her glowing ring.

"You'll get it back," I said quietly. I wasn't sure why I was promising this to her when I planned to kill her.

One moment I was thinking of killing her. The next I was thinking of imbuing her with all her magic and sending her off on a rampage.

"I have enough for now." Her large blue eyes were on the cloudy sky. "I'm not sure all that magic is meant for me."

She didn't think she was capable of managing all that power. "If you want to master your power, you need to ground yourself over the earth. Or use the sea around you. Use the rocks and the soil to absorb the extra charges of magic when it becomes too intense. You let it flow in and out of yourself in an even, steady stream."

She locked her eyes on me and leaned in closer. Tiny droplets of seawater clung to the tips of her long black eyelashes. "And why would you want me to have all that power?"

Good question. "To find the Merrow faster, should this method prove too slow."

Returning her power to her was like watching a dead candle wick spring to life with flame.

The sea wind whipped over my body, a rising gale.

Aenor looked out over the dark water. "I can hear the sound of the Merrow growing a little stronger, but he's still far away."

"How long do you estimate it will take to get there?"

She looked up at the skies. "Considering we're about to get hit with a storm, it could be a while." She frowned at the sail. "This ship could easily capsize."

She had some sort of plan up her sleeve. She thought she might get away from me to work a spell, probably.

"The Isle of Crows is nearby," I said. "I can hear it from here. You can take the ship in to the shoreline while we wait out the storm."

"What's there?"

"A witch's house. And all the crows, obviously, as the name implies." It would do, I supposed. I was used to luxury, but I could be adaptable. I happened to know the witch, and I trusted her well enough.

A gust of wind swelled the sail, and the boat slammed down over a wave.

"Are you doing this?" I leaned back against the boat, steadying myself.

She looked at me with wide eyes. "Doing what?"

With her staged innocent act, I had no doubt she was calling up the storm. She was up to something. I'd be keeping a *very* close eye on her.

But why did she think she could lie to me? Didn't she understand by now that I could make her do what I wanted, tell me what I wanted?

I stared at her, letting my magic boom around her. Her body went rigid as she realized the enchantment spell had invaded her mind again, a poison in her pretty head. She clutched her fists tight, nails piercing her palms, and her jaw tightened.

She stared up at me with such a look of intense hatred that it almost felt like a slap in the face.

"Did you call up this storm, Aenor?" I asked, my voice as icy as the rain.

She grunted with the effort, body straining. She was taking an unexpectedly long time to answer me, and the boat crashed down again on the waves. She lurched in her seat, her skirt riding up her thighs.

Was she starting to learn how to resist my enchantment? The rain fell even harder now, as if her fury alone fueled the storm.

Frustration tightened my chest. I had only a few days left, and I didn't need any more delays.

The boat rose again, cresting a wave. When it smashed down again, Aenor jolted even more. With me in control of her mind, she was no longer able to ride the storm as smoothly.

"Let this be a lesson to you, Aenor. Do not defy me. I control you now." She yanked her skirt down, looking me in the eyes.

The gesture, her hands on her thighs, sent heat racing in my blood.

I shifted sharply where I sat. Why did I find her so alluring? I hadn't thought about sex in centuries, or felt much of anything.

Focus, Salem.

I was in control here. I pinned her with my gaze, and she was helpless before me. A dark smile curled my lips. "Let's try this again. Did you call up the storm?"

At last, the word tumbled out of her mouth. "Yes."

"Why?"

Those nails, jutting into her skin. "I want to be alone. I want to do a spell, to see what the future holds now. I want to see what happens when you get what you want. I want to see what chaos you'll unleash, if the world will burn."

I leaned back, sighing. "How interesting. I'd ask to see this little spell of yours, except I don't care if the world burns. Do you really plan to take me to the Merrow? Or will you try to mislead me?"

"I'm taking you to the Merrow." The answer came out fast and clear, not a moment's hesitation. "I will take you to him, no matter what."

"Good."

"Are you trying to burn the world?" she asked. "Is that your goal?"

I glanced at her hands, now dripping a few droplets of blood. "For the gods' sake, stop doing that with your fingernails."

Pure wrath shone in her eyes.

My chest felt hollow, like someone was carving it out. This invasion of her mind hurt her, and for whatever reason, I didn't like hurting her.

Somehow, she'd infected my mind, just like I'd invaded hers.

I released the enchantment on her. I knew the most important thing. She was definitely taking me where I needed to go.

Then she lunged forward, eyes blazing with fury. "Never do that to me again," she snarled.

Something about the ferocity in her voice, or the blood on her skin, told me I'd agree to her demand.

Her fierce gaze burned into me. "I know what you have planned. Everyone thinks I've gone mad, but I know what you want."

My lip twitched with amusement. "I seriously doubt that, my pet." Only the goddess Anat knew what I truly wanted.

As I watched Aenor, staring out over the stormy sea, it struck me that she seemed painfully *lonely*. When she'd gotten her magic back, she'd called a human friend. Humans died so quickly—a hummingbird's heartbeat and they were gone. Was that whom she attached herself to, only to watch them grow old and die?

What a miserable existence.

If I wasn't careful, I'd start feeling sorry for my captive.

16

AENOR

I guided us toward an island, trying to bury my simmering anger.

Anger would only distract me. If I was going to resist Salem's enchantment, I needed diamond-sharp focus. My resistance had started to work, just a little. Each time he tried to compel me, I was able to resist a little more—the song in my mind drowning out the sound of his magic.

Seawater splashed over my face as we sailed, and I licked my lips. Even in the storm, I could feel the sea was too warm.

Just like in Acre.

Lightning speared the sky above us, and I glanced at Salem. He looked strangely at ease in the heaving boat, the storm winds barely touching him.

My mind started to churn like the ocean around us. Regardless of what the Winter Witch said, I had before me actual proof of a looming threat. The world was heating around us. Was it the Fomorians? I didn't know. I just knew I'd protect the seas until my last dying breath.

As we slammed onto the island's shore, I could hardly

see a thing on it—just rowan trees clawing the sky. The sound of crows cawing wildly around us. When the boat slid onto the shore, I stepped out into the shallow water.

A wave crashed against the shore, the seawater up to my waist now. Ocean spray dappled my skin like a warm balm.

Salem prowled onto the shore, eyes gleaming in the darkness. "Do you have any predictions when this lovely storm you called up might end?"

"Nope."

That was the truth. I didn't have complete control over the storms, and if I did, I'd call up a lightning bolt to strike him. I glanced back at the boat, rocked by the squall.

Salem took off at a fast pace, his head down. I followed behind him, into a wood of rowan and hazel trees. Crows cawed in the boughs above us, their cries piercing the storm. They seemed agitated at our approach, swooping lower around us, grazing my head. I held up my arms to shield myself as they swept overhead. The birds seemed oddly large, their eyes silver.

It was a shame I hadn't managed to call up a storm near an Isle of Charming Kittens.

"Do you have any idea where we're going?" I asked.

"I wouldn't walk without having an idea where I was going. I've been here before."

After a few minutes of walking, I caught sight of a house in the distance. Between the trees, warm light glowed through windowpanes.

We drew closer to the house—which I now saw was a gnarled tree of dark oak, with diamond-pane windows inset in the bark.

A silvery door had been carved into the trunk, and someone had painted the words *Crow Witch* on it in spindly letters.

A knocker hung from the door—a long-fingered silver hand. Salem picked it up to knock.

A few moments later, the door creaked open on its own, revealing a hall carved into the hollow of the tree. While the outside of the tree was only about ten feet wide, the interior somehow opened up into a fairly spacious hall.

From behind the door, a small woman stepped into view. Her long brown hair tumbled over a paisley dress, and a thorny crown rested on her head.

She smiled at Salem. "Welcome. I thought you might be coming, Salem." She looked between us, an eyebrow rising. "I didn't know you'd be bringing your lover. I'd heard all these rumors about how Salem doesn't—"

He shot her a lethal look that had her closing her mouth fast. "Oh, we're not lovers," I said. "At all. He's literally the devil, so..."

She rolled her eyes. "Okay. I see someone got cranky on the boat ride. And what do I call you?"

"Aenor is fine." I added, "Aenor Dahut, House of Meriadoc, Protector of the Seas."

Salem quirked an eyebrow. "So humble, isn't she, my sweet lover?"

I debated whether to explain to her that I was basically Salem's prisoner, but I decided against it.

Salem flashed me a wicked smile. "My darling lover called up this storm because she wanted to be alone with me. But I can pay you very well for a room in your home."

She waved a hand. "Nonsense. You don't need to pay me. Not like I get a lot of company here."

"Two rooms if you have them," I interjected with a smile. "We're not actually lovers."

Salem shrugged, amusement dancing in his eyes.

"Whatever my sweetling wants. Reigning as Protector of the Seas can be a tiring pastime."

He really loved messing with me.

She shook her head. "No. I follow the ancient practices of the Crow Witches, and crows mate for life. I can see the bond between the two of you. You belong together, sharing a room."

Geez, that was a shame, because I was pretty sure we both planned to kill each other.

I sighed. It was all starting to become clear now. So she looked normal, but she was insane.

The woman shrugged. "Also, I only have one extra room, so even without the bond, you're sharing. That's literally the only option. I live in a tree, so... not a ton of rooms in a tree."

Well, it wasn't this woman's fault that Salem was evil. I did my best to smile. "Thank you for letting us stay. I appreciate it."

She motioned to her table. A row of Chinese takeout boxes stood on the oak table, and settings for three. "There's extra food. I thought I might have visitors."

Lanterns hung above the table, and a gust of wind blew into the house, making them swing. I closed the door behind us.

As soon as we stepped further into the small house, a wave of delicious smells greeted me—ginger and garlic.

My mouth watered. "You can get takeout here?"

"I'm a witch. I used a spell."

I pulled out a carved oak chair and sat across from Salem. Angel filled our glasses with red wine. Then she scooped white rice and tofu onto our plates, covered in a thick maroon sauce flecked with chilis.

I felt a bit weird about sitting down at the table soaked in seawater, but these were the only clothes I had.

Turned out that calling up a storm near the Isle of Crows had been the best damn idea I'd had in ages. I'd fill my stomach, then I'd slip away from Salem to cast my spells.

"Now." Angel took a bite of her tofu, then pointed her chopsticks at Salem. "I never believed all those rumors about you. All those sacrifices, all the people you tortured and burned for your amusement in those Jerusalem caves..."

Salem's expression darkened. "It's all true." His voice seemed to come from a million miles away. "I'm skilled in the arts of cruelty beyond anything you could conceive of in your worst nightmares." His glittering gaze slid to me, and I felt like I wanted to shrink away from him. "Aenor has been there, to my rocky hell itself. Perhaps it was the ghosts of wickedness that inspired her to kill her own mother there."

My stomach flipped. "You burned and tortured people for amusement?"

Something pained flashed in his eyes, but then he smiled slowly. "I can give you the details, if you'd like."

Angel shook her head. "Well, I don't know. You seem nice. Not the slaughtering kind."

Lady, your slaydar is way off.

Steam curled from the food, and I scooped a forkful into my mouth. It nearly tasted divine enough to distract me from the conversation we'd just had about burning people for fun.

"So what are you doing here?" Angel asked.

Salem sipped his wine. "My charming lover and I are looking for the Merrow. He has something I want."

She smiled. "Well, whatever it is, I'm sure you have a good reason for wanting to take it from him. You seem like a nice young man."

Completely insane.

I was surprised he just came out with our mission like that, instead of concealing it. But a man as arrogant as Salem maybe didn't worry about anything getting in the way of what he wanted.

She exhaled loudly. "But I must say, it seems a bit dangerous."

"He's already sent his lackeys for us. Any ideas where he has been?"

It struck me for the first time that Salem had an amazing tendency to just tell the truth, however horrible it was. He didn't always tell the whole story—but nor did he conceal his worst faults. He was different from Lyr in that way—Lyr, who cloaked the truth in shadows.

I suspected the parts that Salem hid about himself were the good parts, if there were any.

"I heard his magic through the water," I added. "But we don't know an exact location."

"Could be Mag Mell," she said. "He hangs around there sometimes. But I can't say for sure."

Salem leaned back in his chair, and his easy smile faded. Something had unsettled him like the threat of global destruction had not. "Ah. A place I once knew very well."

Angel pulled a fortune cookie from the center of the table. "Let's see... Will Salem find what he's looking for?" When she pulled out the paper, she smiled. "It says..." She frowned. "'A closed eye gathers no elbows.'"

Salem scrubbed a hand over his mouth. "That makes no sense."

She crumpled it up and threw it away, then narrowed her eyes at Salem. "Forget the cookie. My sense tells me you'll get your thing, whatever it is. Then everything will be all right."

My stomach sank. I could only hope her intuition was as accurate as her *lovers* predictions.

As soon as dinner was over, I'd try my *what if* spell and see what hell Salem would unleash on the world if he got what he wanted.

I'd find out if the Winter Witch had been telling the truth.

17

AENOR

I sipped my wine, surveying the room. With my magic back, my senses felt heightened, and the wind howling outside sounded like a sort of forlorn music. The lantern swung over the table, the light startlingly bright. As I ate, the flavors exploded in my mouth. In the sea, my magic felt more comfortable. On land, I felt like I was drowning in light, in noise.

I drained my glass of wine, muting the flood of sensations a bit. When I finished, I felt a little lightheaded.

Angel smiled at me. "Definitely lovers. I can show you to your room, and you give me your clothes. I'll dry them by the fire while he"—she waggled her eyebrows—"you know, grinds your corn."

Salem's eyes gleamed as he looked at me. "Aenor, my love, the next time you want me to grind your corn, you don't need to go through all the trouble of creating a storm."

I smiled back at him, dripping with sweetness. "Of course, darling. You had me at *I'm skilled in the arts of cruelty.* What girl could resist such charm?"

Then I dropped the smile and did my best to convey "I

will slaughter you in your sleep" with my eyes. Though with my stomach full of delicious Chinese food, it was hard to get a real effective wrath-face going.

Angel rose from her seat. "Well, I'll get you two lovebirds to your room."

She led us to a set of winding stairs that curved upward within the tree. The air smelled heavily of wood and soil. At the top of the stairs, she pushed through a door into a room.

It was a cozy space of dark wood, and a ceiling folded over in a curved peak like leaves pressed against each other. Vines grew from the walls, twinkling with lights and lanterns hung among them.

"Take off your clothes." Angel held out a hand. "I'll dry them by the fire."

I clutched at my soaking shirt. "I'll stay wet tonight, thanks."

Salem arched an eyebrow. My cheeks flared, and I immediately regretted the choice of phrasing.

"Suit yourselves." She crossed out of the room.

Salem pulled off his jacket, his eyes burning as he looked at me. "I guess this is your lucky night, because you may join me in the bed."

"Oh, there will be no corn grinding, Salem. I'm your damn captive. I'm sure you're used to getting whatever you want because of how you look, but it's not happening with me."

The corner of Salem's sensual mouth quirked. "How I look? Please elaborate."

I glared at him. He knew, of course, that his beauty was a destructive force that left a trail of dropped panties in his wake. He was smoldering, masculine perfection. And most women would be thinking about him claiming them up against a wall.

I was not.

Nor was I going to flatter his ego. So instead, I gestured at him and said. "You know, your whole face. Whatever is going on there. How you look."

"I see." A low chuckle.

"It's too fancy for me, frankly, your whole facial region," I added. "I like a simpler face."

What the hells was I babbling about?

He started to unbutton his shirt, and I took in the sight of his chiseled abs, his body thickly corded with muscle. Not a scar on him, despite the physique of a well-trained soldier. My gaze swept down a little lower, where an eight-pointed star beamed on his abs. It seemed to shimmer with starlight. What did that symbol mean?

When I looked at his face again, I caught the smug smile.

"I was just looking at the tattoo," I said.

He laid his shirt on the bed, smoothly folded. He seemed like a tidy sort of person. Everything in the right place...

He turned back to me, and his wings appeared behind him, the dark feathers tinged with golden lantern light. A warm pulse of his magic tingled over my skin. It was like he was trying to take my breath away with just his presence.

His fiery gaze rooted me in place. "You are a very strange woman. You have sparked my curiosity for reasons I don't entirely understand. I think I'd like to explore you more." The timbre of his voice dripped with an erotic promise.

If he *really* wanted to seduce me, all he had to do was use his mind-control power. He'd be claiming me up against the wall in no time.

Why did I keep returning to that image?

His magic skimmed my body, making my wet skin tingle

with heat, every inch of me growing more sensitive. The warm lights sculpted his cheekbones, his muscled body.

"I feel you react to me." His voice was slow, smooth. "Underneath all the rage and the righteousness, a part of you wants me, I think. I'm not sure why that interests me, but it does."

"That's your ego confusing you, my friend." I swallowed hard, my breath coming faster. I wasn't going to look at him shirtless. "I'll take the floor. I'll sleep outside if I have to."

"I can hear your heart beating faster every time I move closer." Then a slow shrug. "But if you want to deprive yourself, who am I to argue?"

His wings disappeared, and he crossed back to the bed. I stared at his powerful back, thickly corded like a warrior's.

I needed to turn the lights out on his physique.

I dimmed the lanterns until the flames flickered down, and the lights in the branches dimmed until complete darkness fell around us. I whispered a sleep spell, one buried in my memory from when my mother used to put me to sleep. A magical lullaby. I felt the room itself relax around me.

I waited for what seemed like ages. At last, the tension in the room began to dissipate, and the room seemed completely still. Salem's breathing slowed.

Carefully, I rose from the floor. In complete silence, I crossed to the door. I inched it open, one millimeter at a time. The hallway was dark now, so I let in no light. My gaze flicked back to Salem. I could hardly see in the dark, but I didn't see any signs of movement.

Carefully, I crept out into the stairwell. This was, maybe, my only chance to get away from him for a few moments. I had two things on the agenda. One, I wanted to get a message to the Merrow. I had a way to send messages through the seawater, though it wasn't discreet. I had to do it when Salem wasn't around.

And two, I needed to see for myself what the future held.

When I'd tiptoed down to the bottom of the stairs, I was disappointed to find that Angel was still awake.

She had laid out a set of tarot cards on the table by the candlelight.

As I crossed through the dining room, she pointed at a card. *The Lovers.* "Ah. Aenor. You see? I was doing your tarot card. This is your future with Salem."

"It really isn't."

She flipped another card. *Death.* Her smile faltered. "That's fine. It just means change." A nervous laugh. "Change is good sometimes."

She flipped another one onto the table, depicting a crumbling tower with flames on the base. *The Tower.*

I frowned at it. "I don't suppose a burning building is good, too?"

"It's definitely destruction—and fire, of course. But, you know, fire can be good! Purification, in some ways. Cleansing..." She sounded unsure of herself.

I found myself moving closer to her, curious about the cards. She flipped another one, and the card depicted two charred bodies on a rock, surrounded by broken bones.

The Conflagration, it read.

Her hand recoiled. She shot me a look of horror.

I didn't know what it was, and I didn't put much stock in Angel's predictions. But the card unnerved me all the same.

"What?" I asked in a small voice. "I've never seen that card before. Is there a positive spin on it?"

She stared at it. "I've never seen it before either." She cocked her head. "It doesn't exist. I mean, it never existed before. But maybe it means something different than what it looks like. Maybe…" She hastily gathered up the cards. "Let's never speak of this again, okay?" Her expression was a forced smile. "Can I get you anything? Tea? Water? Whiskey?"

Nervously, I glanced up at the room I'd left. I had the sense that I definitely wasn't going to get away with my little excursion unnoticed. Salem didn't seem like he missed much—and what was more, Angel's voice wasn't exactly quiet.

Still, he wasn't barging out right now to light me on fire. Might as well take the chance.

"No, thank you. I was just going to nip outside for some fresh air," I said. "I'll be back in just a few minutes."

She'd pulled the Conflagration card from the deck again, staring at it.

I frowned at the macabre card. "You really don't know what that means?"

She cleared her throat. "It is difficult to come up with a positive spin on the charred corpses, and with the crushed bones…" She cleared her throat.

"Right."

With my body buzzing with tension, I crossed to the door. When I pulled it open, a forlorn wind swept over me, chilling me through the damp clothes. Overhead, the crows cawed wildly, wings flapping.

If Salem had been sleeping, he probably wasn't now.

I stepped out into the woods, sniffing the air to smell the sea.

I licked the salt off my lips.

All signs, even Angel's terrible predictions, pointed to destructive fire in my future.

If Lyr found me now—would he still try to wrap that collar around my neck? I wondered if I could call on him if I really needed him. I *thought* I could. He just didn't trust me with all the magic.

When I thought about him, I felt... not much of anything.

The passion just felt *dead*.

I had a weird feeling that Salem was right about my attraction to Lyr. I'd felt lifeless without my magic, and I'd craved oblivion. The silence and peace his presence promised.

But now, I wanted warmth.

The ocean drew me closer with its siren song. What if Angel's cards had some truth in them? Salem and I would never be lovers, of course. But I couldn't deny that he had a seductive allure. His voice, his movements, his smoldering gaze... they all promised an erotic thrill.

He was a dark temptation. I thought I knew what the cards meant. It was simple, really.

If I let his seductive nature distract me, the world would burn.

18

AENOR

The squall still raged, and the wind picked up as I moved closer to the shoreline. The wind whipped at the trees, and when I reached the sand, the salty spume dappled my face.

Aaaah... home.

The wind caressed me as I waded into the sea—the sea that felt too warm for this time of year.

I held out my arms to either side, feeling the waves pound over my legs, my thighs.

First, let's see if the Winter Witch was right about me.

I closed my eyes again. "God of the ocean and sea, show me things that might be. What if I keep my sea magic?"

When I opened my eyes again, I saw a vision gleaming in a sphere. Waves crashed over the fires, and ice spread out on the ocean floor.

The image shimmered away again, and I loosed a breath. That was good, right? If the world could burn, ice and water could put out the fires.

Now what happens if Salem gets what he wants?

"God of the ocean and sea, show me things that might

be. What will happen if Salem frees the woman I buried in the soul cage?"

Sea magic slid over my skin, slick and cold. Then I opened my eyes again to see an image burning in the sphere above me. Fear crawled up my spine.

A world of death had ignited in the bubble. Trees withered; dark smoke curled into the air. In the vision, the seafloor cracked and opened, flames bursting from a crevasse...

The vision spread out of the bubble, bleeding into reality. All around me, the sea began to churn and boil. I stepped back from the ocean as the water burned my skin. Steam rose from the glistening surface. Then, with horror, I watched as the water started to evaporate, leaving behind only dust. Heat scalded my skin as if I stood on the sun. I was on fire, breathless.

The image shimmered away again, and the cold sea crashed against my legs. At last, I exhaled, examining my arms for burns.

Gods have mercy. No wonder the Merrow was trying to kill us. Surely he saw us heading for him, ready to unleash all this destruction on the world.

I glanced behind me at the dark forest. Salem wasn't coming for me, and I had enough time to put my magic to work on a message for the Merrow.

In a storm, you couldn't normally see the phosphorescence glowing in the sea. But with the right magic, you could draw the bioluminescence to you—those little glowing beings that made the dark sea sparkle and glow at night. If you had the right kind of magic, you could use this glittering ocean light to send a message.

"God of the ocean and sea, send my words to the Merrow across the water." As a wave receded, I traced my fingertips over the water, writing, *Merrow*. As my fingertips skimmed the water's surface, phosphorescence beamed beneath it.

I traced another message: *I am the only one who can stop Salem.*

The ocean sucked the words away from me, sending them on their way to the Merrow.

Another wave crashed around me, soaking me completely. As the water calmed, I wrote, *I need the sea glass.*

The sea swallowed this message, too, churning it under the surface.

When the words appeared again, they slid away from me on the ocean's surface. I stared at the faint chinks of light beaming at the sky, drifting farther away from me.

When I turned back for the house, my heart skipped a beat. Salem was watching me, his dark wings cascading behind him. His eyes burned with an icy light.

This wasn't the sophisticated Salem in a mohair suit. This was *Lucifer.* He'd shifted, and short black horns jutted from his bare shoulder blades. He'd come armed with his sword, and that silvery star beamed on his abs. He stood with the preternatural stillness of a demon. Ghostly flames danced in the air around him, warm light carving the masculine planes of his face.

"Aenor," he said in a husky voice. "Planning an escape?"

"I wanted to see what would happen if you achieved your goals. So I did a little spell to see what you have planned. I saw it for myself. The world burning. The sea boiling until it evaporates. That's what happens if we get to the driftwood cage."

The flames rose around him. "Is that what you saw." It sounded like more a statement than a question. Flat. Unimpressed.

"Is that what you want? Are you trying to raise an army of Fomorians to burn the world down?" I took a deep breath, my legs shaking a little. "I think I understand now. All your sophistication—the brandy, the palace, your expensive suits. You're overcompensating, aren't you? You use sophistication to hide what you really are. You just want to burn it all."

Salem lowered his chin, staring at me. Cruel, cold beauty beamed from his face like a star. "I told you, Aenor." Under his silky tone was a sharp blade, a warning. "Do not defy me again. Your mother died fast, but I can make your death a very unpleasant one if I must."

Slowly, the horns and flames receded into the darkness.

The monster who'd killed Mama stood before me.

He might hide his monstrous side with elegance, but I knew what lurked underneath.

19

SALEM

The crows swept over our head, screeching as we reached the house again. We walked in silence as I composed myself. I'd felt about to lose control back there, like I'd wanted to drag her back to the house and never let go of her.

But I hadn't wanted to hurt her. No, I'd wanted to fold her into my wings and pull her close to me.

What a *strange* impulse.

And most perplexing of all, threatening to kill her had felt completely wrong. It was like the words were a toxin poisoning my blood as soon as I'd uttered them. I could feel the threat eating away at me.

Why?

I'd certainly done worse things in my time than kill someone for revenge.

The little vixen had gotten into my head completely, muddling and intoxicating my thoughts. Suddenly, I couldn't make a simple death threat without feeling guilty about it.

Maybe it was that she seemed to understand me... The

sophisticated exterior and the beast who lurked underneath it all. She'd seen right through me, and she found me repulsive. Any sane person would.

My gaze slid to her. Rain poured down her arms and slicked her clothes to her body. She walked hunched, hugging herself.

All I knew now was that I couldn't let her out of my sight.

I could command her right now. *Never leave my side. Don't speak unless you're spoken to. Worship me as a god, Aenor...*

Except I didn't want to invade her mind again, because I didn't want to see her pierce her palms.

When I pushed through the door into the house, I found it silent and dark. The witch had gone to bed, no longer troubling me with her predictions. Aenor walked in silence behind me up the stairs. The urge to strip her wet clothes off her and pull her into my bed to warm her was overwhelming.

In the bedroom, she shot me a furious look, like she was reading my thoughts. "I'll take the floor again."

So she could escape again? Perhaps get a message to Lyr, that tedious, white-haired cock.

Lyr, the morose sea-fuck.

Her *lover.*

The thought of him touching her brought fire to my veins. I'd have to burn something to rid him from my mind. Preferably him.

But while I waited on that, I'd make her bend to my will.

"No, Aenor." My voice sounded rough, desperate. "You have two options now. I can tie you down to sleep, or I can enchant you to stay in this room. Which will it be?"

Her beautiful mouth opened and closed, and she looked stunned for a moment. Then she composed her expression and nodded at the bed. "Fine. Tie me to the bed."

A slow smile. "I thought you'd never ask."

The look she gave me turned my chest to ice, and she crossed to the bed. She lay down on her back, her sea-damp hair and clothes dripping onto the sheets. Droplets of water beaded over goosebumps on her skin. I wanted to warm her.

She raised her arms above her head, wrists near the bedframe. As she did, the look in her eyes was as icy as the water dripping from her skin. Something twisted in my chest as I moved closer to her. I whispered an ancient spell.

I touched her wrists, and ropes of magic twined around them, binding them together.

She despised me for this, but I had to keep her close to me.

I was the one who'd led her into Lyr's arms by ripping her magic from her. He was the allure of death, a promise of reprieve from a life of misery.

"I'm sticking close to you," I barked. It came out sounding more like a threat than I'd meant it to.

I flicked my wrist, and all the lanterns in the room went out. I lay on the bed next to Aenor.

The cold rippled off her, and I let some heat radiate off my body to warm her.

"Don't get anywhere near me," she said through gritted teeth.

"Oh don't worry, Aenor," I murmured. "Not until you beg for it."

"In your dreams."

And wouldn't *that* be a lovely dream. Unfortunately, I couldn't dream anymore. Nothing but a void when I slept.

Really, though, there was nothing like seducing a woman who despised you. When she tried so hard to resist

—then she'd find herself pulling up her skirts a little higher, cheeks flushing as I caressed her thighs. Her legs would open for me, and I'd tease her so slowly, so excruciatingly. As I skimmed my hand over her wet slit, she'd beg me to fuck her. I'd draw it out, waiting till she demanded it of me. I'd make her betray every single objection she had to me until she abandoned herself to pleasure.

That was victory.

It was only a few minutes before I heard Aenor's breathing relax and her heart rate slow down again. I was surprised she'd fallen asleep so fast, close as she was to someone she desperately wanted to kill.

The sound of her breathing lulled me into my own sleep, and I let my body radiate more heat to warm her. I fell into a dreamless sleep, a void.

I woke to find a single light on, glowing over Aenor's smooth, pale skin. She was awake. Still tied up, but staring at me.

"Were you watching me sleep?" I asked. "A bit creepy, don't you think?"

Desire shone in her eyes, and she licked her lips. My pulse raced a little faster. Her pink cheeks were perfection.

She rolled toward me, her legs bent. Her skirt had ridden up high, giving me a view of her pale blue panties. They looked silky, delicate. I wanted to pull them off with my teeth.

My blood roared at the sight of her helpless before me. I could hear her heart beating faster. Her blue eyes were roaming over my body like she was drinking me in.

"Tell me what you want, Aenor," I said quietly.

She met my gaze, a shy smile on her lips. "You."

Oh yes. I pulled her body close to mine, and she wrapped her legs around me. I kissed her deeply. Slowly, I ran one of my hands up her thigh, caressing her. She moaned a little as it slid up further, over her ass. She moved her hips against me, demanding.

I swirled my tongue against hers and teased the hem of her panties. She gasped as I brushed my knuckles over the front of the silk. Hot little minx...

Slowly, at the pace of a glacier, I slid down her panties, pushing them all the way down her legs, then off her ankles. Eyes shining with desire, she rolled onto her back. Her chest rose and fell deeply, breasts straining against her wet shirt.

I knelt between her legs, pulling up her skirt to her waist. With her hands still bound, her knees fell open, inviting me. I could see her arousal and struggled to stay in control. My conquest, spread out before me, ready for me.

Gods, she was perfection, but I'd force myself to take my time. I knelt between her legs, kissing her neck.

She groaned my name. "Salem..." The sound sent warmth spiraling through my chest. I grazed a little hint of teeth over her skin, drawing out the slow kiss on her throat. I flicked my tongue over her skin, tasting her. I'd kiss every inch of her while she screamed my name.

"Salem," she whispered again.

Gods, I loved my name on her lips.

I started to unbutton her shirt and moved my mouth lower over her beautiful breasts. Her nipples were taut, rosy peaks.

I took one of them in my mouth, swirling my tongue over it. Her body was urging me for more, writhing with excitement.

"Salem, please..."

"Please, what?" I purred.

I stroked my fingertips down to the slickness between her thighs, sliding my finger in light circles.

As I teased her, I whispered, "Ask me for what you want, Aenor."

I kept my touch so light that she seemed like she was vibrating with desire. Her body craved satiation, and I was drawing it out.

"I want you, Salem," she said at last.

At that, I lost all control I had. I pulled off my pants, ready to slide in—

I woke from the dream with a start. Immediately, disappointment hit me like a cold fist. A chill washed over me.

What in the rockiest pits of hell...

First of all, I didn't dream. I hadn't dreamt since before I'd been cursed, eons ago. I hadn't dreamt since humans still lived in caves, trying to kill each other with animal bones.

Second of all, I didn't *feel* things anymore, and now I was feeling things.

And, most importantly, why was my mind on Aenor's body? I was so close to finding the soul cage, and I'd become full of distractions.

Night still cloaked the room in darkness, but already I knew what time it was. Like clockwork, I always woke just before dawn. Rarely did I miss the first blush of morning light, no matter where I was in the world.

A cold sort of horror was building inside me as I realized I'd moved location in my sleep.

Beneath my body, I felt a hard floor instead of the bed. A single, thin ray of milky light beamed from under the crack in the door. Next to me.

Somehow, without realizing it, I'd shifted onto the floor just by the door. I'd slept in front of it. It was like... like I was guarding the room. It was the primitive behavior of an animal trying to protect its mate.

Dread crawled over my skin, but I wouldn't let myself delve too deeply into what this meant.

We simply had to get out of here. We had to keep going, and I wouldn't think about Aenor anymore. I wouldn't look at her.

I had to kill the electric attraction I felt between us.

I'd simply make her hate me more than she already did. That wouldn't be difficult, of course. All I had to do was tell her the rest of the truth about myself. Her revulsion for me would be complete.

I snapped my fingers, and flames ignited where the torches hung in sconces.

Aenor gasped, her eyes snapping open. "Gods have mercy..." she muttered. "I was having a *really* good dream."

For just a moment, I was tempted to ask what it was, sparked with the hope that it was about me. Did we have the same dream?

Instead, I snapped my fingers again, popping the ropes of magic off her hands.

She sat up, rubbing her wrists. "Why are you waking me in the middle of the night?"

Tension tightly coiled my body, and I pulled on my shirt, smoothing it out. "Dawn is breaking. The storm should be over now."

I turned away from her, unwilling to look at her long eyelashes as she blinked.

Already, my mind was on Mag Mell.

After all these years, I'd be going back.

It had been millennia since I'd ruled there, but when I closed my eyes at night, before I fell asleep, I could still see the way the sunlight streamed through the oak leaves. I could smell the richness of the soil and feel the heavy air on my skin. My second paradise, and second exile.

I'd poisoned it all, of course.

"The sun is rising soon, and I won't miss dawn," I said. "You threw us off course already with the storm you called up, and I won't wait any longer. Call your magic boat. We're going to the Merrow."

She slid her perfect legs over the side of the bed, giving me a sweet smile I knew she didn't mean. "Why the rush? I thought we were getting along so well after you tied me to the bed."

20

AENOR

I sat across from Salem in the boat, blinking in the morning light. Coral streaked a periwinkle sky.

Before, he'd seemed so curious about me, staring at me with intensity. Now, it seemed like he didn't want to look at me at all. Like I disturbed him.

Something about my understanding of Salem didn't seem complete. I was missing something.

I supposed it wouldn't kill me to know Salem a little better—what made him tick.

Right now, he seemed entranced by the sunrise as we sailed on the calm seas.

A gust of wind blew my hair into my face, the ruddy sunlight tingeing it with a violet hue. Peaceful. I could even hear the sea's song lulling us along.

I sipped my coffee, the steam warming my face. Angel had given that to us before we left. She'd also handed over a basket of hot, buttered scones along with some kind of warning about burning to death. It had been a confusing mixture of comfort and terror.

She needn't have continued to warn me. By now, the doom prophecies were clear.

I sighed and reached into the basket to pull out another scone. As I did, I realized what it was—the thing that didn't fit with Salem's entire malign presence. His whole *I am an evil torturer who cares for no one* vibe.

"What's your cat's name?" I asked.

"Aurora," he murmured absent-mindedly, still looking at the sky.

Then he snapped out of his trance and shot me an irritated look. It was like I'd just manipulated a secret out of him.

"If you want to light the world on fire, why do you have a cat?" I asked.

He stared at me. "I fail to see the connection."

"You have a well-looked-after cat, who you've named and everything. She's groomed and healthy, and she clearly loves you by the way she was rubbing your legs." I tapped my fingers on my knees. "Now what I don't get is why look after a cat if you plan to destroy the world? You love that cat."

"Don't make the mistake of thinking I can love. Or that underneath it all I'm *nice,* Aenor. I'm not. I *am* Lucifer." The rosy sunlight glinted in his eyes as he leaned back against the boat.

"I just wouldn't imagine the devil would have a cat." I frowned. "Or perhaps it fits."

"Let me remind you who I am." He stared at me, fury in his eyes. I felt his magic booming around me, reverberating in the inside of my mind. He was doing it again, godsdamn him. I tried to drown out the sound of his magic with a tune in my mind.

"I need to know. I'm after something I've wanted for

millennia, and I need to know. Are we still going to the Merrow?"

"Yes," I said through gritted teeth.

"And the Merrow knows where the soul cage is?"

"Yes."

Slowly, he released the magical hold on my mind. He looked agitated, like the whole experience disturbed him as much as it disturbed me.

I sipped my coffee, unwilling to let him see that he'd rattled me. "Don't worry, Salem—I don't think you're nice at all. I think you're evil to your bones, and the world would be better off if you were dead. But I also think maybe you like company. And if you've been looking after a cat, maybe you don't want your cat to die in an inferno of your making."

The boat rocked gently over the waves.

"You're trying to humanize me. Stop it." Golden sunlight sparked off the blue in his eyes. "Can you hear the Merrow now?"

I trailed my fingertips in the water, reassured by the Merrow's song floating through the waves. "Yes. His song has grown a little stronger. Any idea how far we are from Mag Mell?"

"Only a few hours."

I narrowed my eyes at him. "Not that I'd expect you to care, but I'd like you to know that I have better things to do than burn the world down with you."

"Ah. Yes. I'm sure you could be having scintillating conversations with Lyr at this very moment while he wanders in and out of a death realm." He pulled out his flask of brandy. "Can he actually speak, or does he just grunt and break things?"

He almost sounded jealous, but he was getting me off my main point. "Exactly why do you want to burn the world down, Salem? What do you get out of it? Can't you just enjoy your brandy and your fancy suits and your mansion? You could seduce any woman you wanted to."

"*Any?*" He managed to imbue the single word with an ocean of innuendo.

At least I'd pulled his attention off the sky again, and he was focused on me.

I straightened. "Not me, obviously. But why can't you just enjoy all that? What more do you want?"

That little smile disappeared from his lips. "I can't enjoy any of it. I don't feel anything, Aenor. Or at least I haven't—" He seemed to catch himself, and he stopped. Then he leaned back in the boat, elbows over the edge like he was completely at ease. The wind ruffled his hair.

"You really think you can convince me to change my ways?" Amusement gleamed in his eyes. "You think you can find the nice devil underneath it all? That I should just be happy with what I have? Do you have any idea how long I've been seeking my destiny?"

I shrugged. "Maybe I sense you want more than just destruction. You're longing for something else."

"I am. But it's not love, if that's what you think. I *can't* love. I never could. I feel animal impulses, nothing more. There's nothing to redeem in me, Aenor." A wicked curl of his lips. "Now I have an idea. Perhaps it's time you got to know the real me, and I'll disabuse you of this time-wasting venture."

"I don't have a choice about this, do I? Given that we're stuck in a small boat together."

"I was the second king to rule Mag Mell."

"I saw that during my research."

"When we get there, we will find it full of all sorts of depravity. Intoxicating wine and food, dancing and fucking.

It's where fae go for sexual gratification, to have their most debased fantasies fulfilled."

That was his kingdom. Of course it was. "Can't wait."

"But once, it was a perfect paradise for the fae. Dancing, singing, poetry, cathedrals of oak trees that strained to the skies. But that wasn't enough for me. Nothing was ever enough for me, because I always felt like I was falling. I changed paradise. I started turning it into the den of iniquity and depravity that you'll find today. And for that, I was cast out by the good people of Mag Mell. But it was too late, because once the flames of my sin had begun to spread, they caught on like wildfire. Mag Mell was never the same. I went back sometimes over the years to enjoy myself, but I didn't really need it. I had my own pleasures halfway across the world."

First cast from the heavens, then from his own kingdom. "And why wasn't it enough for you?"

"I could never fill the dark void in my chest, the feeling that I was plummeting." The illusion of flames licked at the air around him, casting sinister shadows beneath his face. "In the heavens, I'd been a god, a leader among the celestial beings. I'd led the losing side in the war. And when I fell, Aenor, it was like my soul was ripped out of my body." Fury danced in his eyes. "I wanted to fill the chasm with fighting and fucking and getting everything I wanted, controlling everyone."

I took a deep breath. "Okay, so you're awful. I still don't get it. Why burn the world now? Connect the dots for me like I'm an idiot."

He hesitated for a moment, then said, "I thrive in fire, Aenor. When I was banished from Mag Mell, I wandered across the world, growing more and more bestial. I was insatiable for the torment of others. I roamed across the earth until I found that little cave near Jerusalem, where I'd stare at the evening sky every night, my former home. Emptiness ate at me. During the day I reveled in two things: seduction and death. I created hell on earth in a place called Gehenna, near the field of blood. Women offered their bodies to me. Other supplicants burned their loved ones, offerings to their god. Sacrifices—to me. They killed their own children to please me. To get my blessing. And I *liked* it. I grew strong off it."

Nausea spread in the pit of my stomach. He truly was more twisted than I'd understood.

I didn't really want to hear more, but I had to. "And you want that from the whole world? It will make you happy?"

"It was my dark paradise. Humans call it Gehenna; some call it hell. You've seen the paintings humans have made, the stained-glass windows showing the flames of hell? They put them in the western windows of churches to catch the wild twilight rays. That's my light, flames dancing on the glass to terrify people. I inspired that. That is my legacy. Thousands of years of human tribes killing each other, cursing each other in my name. Lucifer. Light-bringer. Tormenter. *That's* my legacy."

I hugged myself, chilled to the bone. "Why did people sacrifice to you?"

A slow shrug. "They thought me a god. Why wouldn't they? I had wings, and magical powers. I didn't disabuse them of this notion. And after all, I *had* been a god. I'm practically one now. So they burned their own in offerings to me, hoping to win my favor. In that cave where we encountered your mother, the victims' screams echoed off the cave walls. They used drums to drown the cries out. You can hear them, can't you? In my magic? But they needn't have drowned out the screams on my account. I thrived on agony. That's who I am, Aenor. I torment."

My blood had turned to ice. "Yeah. I can hear the drums."

He flashed me a sly, mirthless smile. "I'm a jealous god. If you're going to make a sacrifice, make it to me."

Something felt off in this story, but I couldn't pinpoint what it was.

"You're not a god anymore."

"I will be," he shot back.

Interesting. "Oh really? Is that your destiny?"

As the words were out of my mouth, an unfamiliar magic slipped over my skin, stroking up my bare legs.

What had we been talking about? I couldn't remember. The air felt humid now, scented of gardenias. I sighed, all my fears evaporating.

I stared at Salem, at the dawn light that sculpted his perfect, sharp jaw line, his cheekbones. I felt like all the chilling things he'd just been talking about evaporated as well, leaving behind only his pure physical perfection.

Why was he transfixing me so much right now? He was a *psychopath,* dammit.

Some kind of seductive magic was at work.

21

AENOR

He stared back at me, the wind sweeping over him. Slowly, he took a sip from his flask. He leaned closer, eyes boring into me, like he was daring me to do something. The air seemed heavy and full of erotic tension.

"Stop it," I snapped.

Only this time, he didn't stop.

My pulse raced, nipples tightening in response. I felt acutely aware of the feel of my clothes on my body, like an excruciating sexual torture. I closed my eyes, trying not to think about Salem. I repeated the word *psychopath* in my mind. I thought of his torture cave, the scent of sulfur and burning flesh. Passion killer.

When I opened my eyes again, I forgot all those unpleasant things and remembered how he'd looked without his shirt on... a chiseled god. I crossed my legs, clenching my thighs. *One... two... three.* I wasn't sure if I was trying to restrain myself or satiate myself.

A deep, sexual ache built in my core, and the wind felt

like it was licking my skin. What if I lifted my skirt and touched myself...

Stop it, Aenor. I despised him.

But my breath was speeding up, wild need quaking through my body.

Unless... unless I could use this.

He obviously wanted me. I'd seen him looking at my body, at my mouth. I saw the way he gazed at me hungrily when he'd tied me up, like he wanted to lick the seawater off every inch of my body until I screamed.

What if I could seduce him? What if I could keep him happy enough that he'd forget his whole plan? If he was overcome with pleasure, he wouldn't need to burn the world.

Yes... This all made sense.

If I crawled into his lap and unbuttoned my top...

My breasts felt full and heavy, aching for his hands. It was as if invisible tongues were licking at my nipples, stroking me to a frenzy.

A hot ache between my legs forced them open. The boat rocked back and forth, back and forth... I fought the urge to slide my hand into my panties right in front of him. My hips rocked on the seat.

Salem was just looking at me, like he knew exactly what he was doing. He was *tormenting* me. That was what he did. He tormented people.

And gods help me, I liked it right now.

When I felt the cold sea air on my chest, I became aware that I was unbuttoning my top, legs splayed while I stared at him.

No. *No, Aenor.* He must have been invading my mind.

I stopped unbuttoning halfway down, the tops of my breasts exposed. The feel of my silky shirt against my skin was an excruciating erotic torture. One by one, I started fastening the buttons again.

"Stop doing that," I said. I tried for that commanding voice again, but it came out pleading.

"What is it you imagine I'm doing to you?" His deep voice carried an erotic promise. "I'd love to know."

"Stop making me feel things."

"I assure you I'm doing no such thing, but that is fascinating." His eyes danced, gaze sliding down my body. "And where are you feeling things?"

Cold air on my thighs told me I had hiked up my skirt, and the wind kissed my panties. *Gods have mercy.* I yanked the hem of my skirt down again, a furious blush burning my cheeks. I kept the hem firmly in my grip.

Salem rose where he stood, staying steady in the boat. Then he crossed to me, eyes locked on me like a hunter.

My breath shuddered as he leaned down, hands on either side of me. He was gripping the side of the boat behind me, boxing me in.

He moved in close, giving me a slow smile. With his mouth next to my ear, he whispered in a low voice, "I know you're keeping secrets from me, Aenor. You have something planned. You're conspiring against me." His velvet-smooth voice stroked my body. It was a sensual, dangerous touch that skimmed the apex of my thighs.

My knees opened wider, and I felt the cold air between my legs again. My shirt had been pulled up again. My eyes were wide as I looked at him.

"You've been bad, haven't you?" he purred, still boxing me in.

Wild need burned all rational thought from my mind. A sexual ache swooped between my legs.

All I knew was that I was too hot in my shirt. The cold

sea wind whispered over my bare breasts as I took it off. He lowered his eyes, and a wicked smile curled his lips. His body had gone completely tense, muscles taut.

"Bad? I don't know what you're talking about," I whispered.

His magic slid between my legs, a phantom licking that grew stronger. My mind went blank, and liquid heat rushed through my body.

His lust magic had curled around me completely, until everything felt like sexual torment—the rocking of the boat, the feel of the wood beneath my bare legs. The wind tingling over my exposed skin.

I wanted to touch myself so badly that I could hardly resist it. I looked up into his eyes, and they shifted from blue to a deep red.

I was so turned on that I could hardly protest when he picked me up by the waist and turned me around to face the sea. I knelt on the seat, leaning over the side. Salem leaned down behind me, his powerful body pressed against mine, warming my naked back. He slid his hand down my side to keep me in place where he wanted me. Raw, masculine power radiated off him.

Molding himself around my body, he cupped my breasts, thumbs skimming my nipples. He leaned down next to my ear. "You have been lying to me. Haven't you?" His deep voice trembled over my skin. "We'll have to do something about that. I'll find out the truth from you, I think."

"Mmmm..."

He slid his hands further down my body till they reached the hem of my skirt. Then he yanked it all the way up to my waist. He leaned over me again, one of his hands covering mine where I gripped the side of the boat.

Slowly, he traced his finger just inside the top of my panties, leaving a hot trail of tingles as he swept from one side to another. My entire body was exquisitely sensitive, and I gasped at his light touch. I shuddered, moving my hips back against him. I could feel his length pressing against me.

Slowly, he hooked his finger into the side of my underwear, teasing me. "Don't ever think you can lie to me, Aenor."

He pulled my panties down sharply, exposing me completely.

I gasped as the wind hit me.

I was desperate for him to touch me. Vaguely, I was aware that I needed to pull my skirt down, but I couldn't bring myself to do it. So I knelt there, naked and turned on before him.

He slid a hand down my back, guiding me to lean on the side of the boat. My breasts pressed against the damp wood, my bare ass in the air. I knew he was enjoying the sight of me, turned on and submissive before him.

I gasped when his hand came down *hard* on my bottom, the sound of the smack echoing through the air. It hurt for a moment, and then it felt like a wild pleasure rippling through me. He hit me again, pleasure arcing through me at the smack. Gods, I *liked* this? I was so turned on that every time he hit me I could feel my nipples tightening more to sensitive points, my sex clenching.

He smacked my bottom again, and again, until I was sure my skin had gone pink. Each time, I gasped with pleasure. He had complete control over me, and he knew it.

Now, his hand was moving lower when he smacked me.

When he struck me between my legs, I moaned with

pleasure—a wild sound that came from some ancient, animal part of my brain.

"Please," I whispered, not even sure what I was asking for. I ached for him, and I didn't care what the consequences were anymore.

The hand on my back slid up to grab my hair. His other moved down to my inner thighs. His painfully light touch was pure torture—a worse punishment than anything else. I needed him to slide in and out of me, filling me.

Instead, he stroked slow circles on my upper thighs. My legs widened. I moved my hips, trying to demand more from him. I knew he could see exactly how turned on I was.

Writhing with need, I craved satiation.

At last, he reached the apex of my thighs—but he was still touching me lightly. Slowly, he brushed his finger over my sex. My hips bucked. I'd do anything for release. I no longer cared that I hated him, or that I'd vowed to kill him.

"Please," I said again.

"I told you, Aenor," he purred. "You despise me, but I told you I'd make you'd beg for it, didn't I?"

Fill me, Salem.

"Aenor…" His voice sent a fresh rush of molten desire pounding through my body. "You're mine now. Tell me what you want."

I needed him to fill me now so desperately that I couldn't even form the words. I moaned, ravenous with animal desire. Slowly, he slid a finger into me, and I clenched around him. He pulsed it in and out, and I moved back against his hand.

No. No.

None of this was happening. Was it?

None of this was actually happening.

The burning. The screams. The *drum.*

I could hear the drum now. If I gave in to him, everything burned.

As I let Salem fuck me, the sea began to boil, seawater evaporating into reddening skies. Fire seared the landscape on a distant island, trees blazing like torches.

This wasn't happening.

This wasn't real.

22

SALEM

I stared across the boat at Aenor. Her blue eyes seemed to glaze over, her mouth open. She gaped dumbly at the ocean water like she'd been lulled into a magical stupor. I thought, perhaps, she might even be drooling. Something had just struck her dumb, but I had no idea what it was. She'd just stopped speaking mid-conversation.

Was she hallucinating?

She *really* didn't look quite herself right now.

"Aenor?" I said.

The breeze lifted her hair in front of her face, and she didn't move a hand to swat it away. Her ceramic mug of coffee slid out of her fingertips, smashing on the floor of the boat. She didn't react a bit. I could only hear that her heart was racing. Her cheeks had gone flushed.

What in the gods' names was she thinking about?

"Aenor!" I said again.

Her gaze snapped to me. She was alert now, and she licked her lips. Her cheeks had gone pink. She actually looked like she desired me, and my heart sped up.

I knew that look well, but I hadn't expected to see it from

her. She crossed her legs tight, like she was trying to resist while she stared at me. Gods, the look in her eyes should have made me delighted, but it felt like ice shattering in my heart. No matter what, she couldn't look at me like that forever. It wouldn't last.

She rose from her seat and crossed the rocking boat to me. "I'm feeling a little cold."

Her gaze roamed down my body, then up again to my face, eyes half-lidded with desire.

Gods, she was perfect.

She trailed one fingertip down her chest, like she was tracing a raindrop down her body. She *wanted* me, and that was all I needed to know. Already, I was hard.

I grabbed her by the waist, pulling her into my lap, and she didn't resist. I swept my gaze over her curvy body, already imagining ripping her clothes off her. I wanted to kiss her between her legs until she moaned my name.

"What are you doing?" she whispered, but she wasn't pulling away.

She gave in to me as I pulled her closer and kissed her throat. Her neck arched as I swirled my tongue over it.

Ever so slightly, her knees were opening a little in an invitation. I wanted her naked, now, spread before me like a prize, but I wasn't going to rush it. I was going to take my time with her.

I kissed her neck more deeply. Slowly, I stroked my hand up her inner thigh. I brushed lazy circles, higher and higher, coaxing her legs open wider. She was quickly losing the battle with any resistance she might have. She was *mine.*

When I gently stroked my knuckles over the front of her silky knickers, she took a deep, trembling breath. I could feel her arousal even now, hot and wet beneath the silk.

I pulled my hand away, and she gasped like she was shocked. "Salem," she whispered, a blush on her cheeks.

"Yes?" I murmured. *Let's hear you say what you want.*

Staring into my eyes, she started unbuttoning her shirt, until her plump breasts were exposed before me. I kissed them, gently, then took her nipple in my mouth, sucking on it. My tongue swirled as I tasted her.

She writhed in my lap, head back with ecstasy. When I glanced up at her face, I found her rosy lips parted with desire. The sunlight bathed her skin in gold, so beautiful that it was like a knife in my heart.

I slid my hand under her skirt, brushing my knuckles against her heat again.

Slowly, I pulled her panties down, dragging them down her legs, off her ankles.

She spread her legs wider, her skirt riding up until I could see all of her. Her desire for me was apparent. *Hot little minx.*

I'd draw out her excitement as long as I could. Then I'd fuck her until she forgot her own name.

I stroked my fingertips between her legs again, almost groaning at her slickness. She went wild with desire, her breasts brushing against me. She shifted against my hard length. I slid a finger into her.

"What do you want, Aenor?" I whispered low in her ear. "Say it."

I already knew what she really needed. She needed me to spread her legs and fuck her tight little hole until—

She shifted, straddling me, eyes blazing with fury.

She *definitely* did not look turned on anymore. Though, admittedly, I still was.

I was so intent on the sudden rage in her face that I nearly didn't see the piece of sea glass she'd pressed against my chest—sharp as a blade. It was the same perfect blue as her eyes. "I want you dead, my soulmate. And I'm the only one who can kill you."

"What are you doing?"

Where had the bloody sea glass come from? What was going on?

Her face only inches from mine, she plunged the shard into my heart. Her eyes locked on mine, brimming with tears now, and I could feel the life seeping out of me. A tear streaked down her cheek, and I wanted to brush it away, but I was dying.

My heart had stopped, and my mind whirled with darkness. I was falling again. Plummeting.

So close to achieving my destiny, and it was all over.

The evening star burned out for good.

~

WHEN THE VISION CLEARED, I found that Aenor and I were staring at each other, slightly dumbstruck.

We were alive in a boat on the calm sea, and, regrettably, fully clothed. No one was fucking anyone. On the plus side, nor was anyone murdering me with sea glass.

"What the fuck was that?" I shouted. Had I ever been this rattled?

She blinked at me. "I just had a horrific vision of my worst fear."

"What was it?"

Her cheeks were red. "Never mind that. I think the Ollephest might be near. You know, the thing that killed Ossian's mate. It shows you your worst—"

A loud roaring interrupted her, and a scaled creature rose from the water behind her. Its jaw alone was nearly the size of the boat, and its dark eyes were intent on Aenor. The blood of some other victim dripped from its teeth.

Ah. Yes. The Ollephest. I supposed *that* explained the visions.

Aenor stared up at him, and a surge of protective rage erupted in me. I felt my wings shoot out behind my back as I took on my true form. I pulled out Lightbringer, flames blazing from the steel. My wings beat the air fast, lifting me into the sky above the boat.

The Ollephest swerved along the waves, its body moving along with them. It shone in the morning sun with brilliant blue and green scales.

As the creature opened its mouth above Aenor, I swooped and brought my sword down hard into its neck. The thing shrieked, but it was far too big for me to sever its neck completely.

It swung its head toward me, fangs glinting in the sun. I drove my sword into its eye.

Roaring, the creature swiped at me with a taloned hand, carving into my wing.

The pain was nearly indescribable, searing and deeply invasive. It was like a burning nail being scraped across a naked bone.

I gripped Lightbringer hard, fighting to keep control so I could kill the thing. Arcing around its head, I drove my blade into its other eye, blinding it.

Good. Nearly done.

But its attacks were growing more frantic, talons swiping wildly at anything around it. Clearly, I knew how to injure him, but how did I *kill* him?

I looked below me to find that the sea level seemed to have receded, pulling the monster away from me.

Aenor looked minute in her boat so far below me. It took me a moment to realize she was controlling the sea.

She gazed up at me, her eyes bright blue. I started to swoop lower, but my shattered wing made my flight irregular. Each beat of my wings was like a thousand blades pushed into my body. Still, if I could get to Aenor, I could lift her away from the monster. I dove for her and wrapped my arms tight around her waist, gripping her to my body.

My wings thumped the air, and as I lifted her, she curled her arms around my neck, holding on tight. When she wrapped her legs around my waist, an ember ignited in my heart.

The feeling was short-lived, because the monster slammed its spiked tail into us with the force of a bomb. My bones shook, wing bones cracking harder. It was like being hit with a three-hundred-mile-per-hour train. I lost my grip on Aenor, and she lost hers on me. Fear coiled through my heart.

The wind rushed over me as we tumbled back into the frothing sea. I hit the water hard, my wing snapping with a searing pain, and I sank deep under the water.

The sea was churning now, and I couldn't tell which was up or down. My lungs started to burn as I scrambled for control, searching for Aenor under the water. Unlike me, she'd be fine under there.

As long as the creature wasn't raking a claw through her body.

Something like panic was building in me as I fought my way to the surface, pushing out the pain in my wing. My lungs burned. I couldn't die, but I could feel a world of pain. Especially if something happened to Aenor...

Was that a scream I heard through the water? Panic, now clear and real, burned hotter in my mind. Where was the source of light? Was I swimming deeper under the water, or heading for the surface?

At all costs, I had to get to her. Because even as I scrambled for the surface of the water, the horrible truth was dawning on me—the reason her pain bothered me, the reason I couldn't kill her. The reason blind fear drove me to protect her at all costs.

The Ollephest showed you your worst fears. And my worst fear had manifested before me. Because only one person could kill me, and that person was my mate.

This was the dark, jagged thought I'd buried since I first met her. Now, the truth was ripping its way up to the surface of my mind.

Aenor was my mate. I'd scented it on her the moment I first met her. That intoxicating smell of brine and wildflowers and an animal instinct that wanted me to keep her close. The force of nature that compelled me to sleep in front of a door while she rested.

Instinct propelled me. Every cell in my body screamed at me to keep her safe, that I'd just dragged her into a world of danger.

At last, I fought my way up to the surface of the sea, gasping for air. I searched for Aenor, only to find that the monster had grasped her in its talons.

Bright, hot rage exploded in my mind, and I started to beat my wings under the sea. But the water fractured my shattered wing, and I'd lost Lightbringer.

For just a moment, Aenor caught my gaze, looking almost apologetic. What was she sorry for?

A deep roar rumbled through my bones. It wasn't the beast. A wave, tall as a mountain and sparkling with sunlight, rushed for us.

That was Aenor's work, and it looked like pure destruction. Fucking glorious.

With my broken wing, I didn't have time to get out of its way before it slammed down on me, the sea grinding me into itself like flour in a mill. Thousands of tons of water churned me under, crushing me. It felt like my body was ripping in half.

Until I was on land, I wouldn't be able to heal myself properly.

And yet—all I could think was that I hoped Aenor had pulled herself away from the creature.

23

AENOR

The wave I'd created had ripped me from the monster's grasp, but his magic still shrieked through the water. He wasn't far, his vibrations trembling cold over my body. My blood turned to ice.

I swam in the depths of the raging sea, searching for Salem. The waters churned in whorls and vortices, life rushing around me. I could stay here forever if I didn't have a fae to kill.

For some strange reason, the thought of killing Salem spread frosty blooms of dread through my chest. Almost like I didn't *want* to kill him.

I searched the murky water for Salem, blood clouding around me. Where was it all coming from?

I looked down at my body, at the brutal gashes on my arm and leg. The Ollephest had sunk his talons into my flesh, ripping it right open. With all the adrenaline pumping, I hadn't noticed it before. Now, the sight of it sent alarm bells ringing in my mind. As soon as I saw bone exposed through my flesh, pain screamed up my arm and my leg.

I whirled around, trying to find Salem.

At last, in the ocean's gloom, I saw him. His body glowed like a distant star. I'd seen that before, hadn't I? A vision or a dream... A silver sphere in the dark seawaters, as beautiful and stark as the dawn of the universe. The cold perfection of the evening star.

The monster's screaming focused my attention again into a diamond-sharp point. Spurred into action, I shot through the ocean, the water rushing around me. The pain in my limbs was forgotten.

As I swam closer to Salem, I grimaced. His wing had been nearly torn in half. He was fighting against the waves, his wing ripping further.

Despite everything I knew about him, my heart constricted a little at the sight of the blood clouding around him. He was swimming for the surface, but his broken wing dragged in the water.

When I reached him, I gripped him around the waist and kicked. His muscular arms wrapped around me, and his body heated me in the water. His heart reverberated in my chest.

When he met my gaze, I saw his eyes had gone a murky red. Unlike me, he needed air. He wouldn't die—not without the sea glass in my hands—but his lungs probably felt like they were on fire.

As I swam, the Ollephest's shrieking grew louder. He was closing in on us. Like me, he might hunt underwater by sound. I closed my eyes, trying to tune in to the feel of solid land anywhere nearby.

After a moment, I felt it.

An island close by, solid in the raging sea. Less than a mile away, I thought. We just needed to get there, drag ourselves onto land. Dizziness whirled in my head as blood flowed out of me.

I closed my eyes as I tuned into the water. Letting my sea magic course through my body, I created a fast current. Roiling around us, the current began ushering us to the shore.

As the cool waters carried us, my mind was going darker, cloudier. I rested my head on Salem's chest, and he pulled me in close. While the sea carried us, my legs tingled with pins and needles, and my body started to feel cold. Slowly, my hands were growing numb.

But through my mental fog, I could tell the screeching of the Ollephest was growing more distant. *Everything* was growing more distant, and I started losing my grip on Salem. He still held me close, his heart beating against mine, body radiating warmth. His grip on me was firm, unwavering, and gentle as a father holding a child. Like I was his salvation. Of course, he didn't know what I had planned for him...

I was dimly aware of the feel of the air, and of Salem carrying me from the water. His powerful arms curled around me. The saltwater stung my wounds. I could no longer feel my legs.

When I opened my eyes, I saw droplets of seawater beading on his skin. He looked determined, and laid me down gently in his lap.

"I'm fine," I said, but my eyes were closing again, and my head rested on his firm chest.

～

WHEN I OPENED MY EYES, I saw him kneeling over me. I was flat on my back, on something soft. He pressed his hand against my chest, and heat radiated out from his fingertips.

My gaze landed on his wing, brutally broken, feathers cracked in two.

"What are you doing?" I asked.

His dusky gaze met mine, the colors in his eyes shifting from blue to violet-grey. Heat beamed out from his hand on my chest, washing over me. "You were losing too much blood. This will help, a little."

Seawater ran down his golden skin in rivulets as he healed me. He was a healer? I didn't expect that in the skillset of a rampant sadist.

Mostly—right now—I was doing my best to ignore the fact that his hand rested between my breasts. His eyes were on my wounds, his brow furrowed.

As his magic slid along my body, the warmth carried along with it emotions. A sense of longing, maybe.

He yearned for something always out of his grasp, a heat and brightness he'd once possessed. He no longer felt complete, and all the fire in the world couldn't keep him warm.

As his magic coiled around my body, his torment moved along with it. The sound of drums beat in my mind.

This was too close, too intimate, until the feeling of longing dimmed. Slowly, a deep sense of relaxation took over, and the pain ebbed.

My eyes fluttered closed for a moment, and I felt Salem's hand pull away. When I opened my eyes again, he was kneeling above me, holding moss and strips of cloth. His wing looked half torn from his body.

Kneeling by my side, he gently lifted my arm. This was all getting too... close.

"I can bandage myself," I muttered.

"Aenor, you're not going to bandage yourself up with a single arm. I need to get this done properly, since you've already inconvenienced me enough by allowing the Olle-phest to shred your limbs open."

"How rude of me," I said wearily. "And you allowed your wing to get shredded. Does it hurt?"

"Are you concerned for my well-being? I'm touched."

"It's just a detached curiosity. I've never had wings before, so I don't know what they feel like."

"It hurts like you wouldn't believe, but I can heal myself once I'm done here."

He pressed the moss against my arm, then bound it in the cloth. Sunlight streamed over him, gilding his shoulders and wings. It took me a moment to realize he'd ripped up his own shirt to make the bandages. He knelt bare-chested, the eight-pointed star beaming on his abs.

A little light flitted around him—a bright sphere with a twilight sheen. It flitted and bobbed around his head like a lightning bug.

"What is that?" I asked.

He went still for a moment, watching it. As he did, his chest went taut, and a muscle twitched in his jaw. Whatever that little thing was, it unsettled him.

He turned to me again. His expression was sharp, even though his hands were gentle as he wrapped a strip of cloth around my arm. "Never mind that little bug. I'm fixing you only so you can bring me where I need to go. You'll need to rest now. As soon as you can produce this soul cage, it will all be over. We will never need to see each other again."

It will all be over when you're dead.

"What did you see?" I asked. "What's the worst fear that the Ollephest showed you?"

He paused in his bandage wrapping and stared at me. "Death."

Surprise flickered, and maybe a little guilt. "That's it? You're scared of death." It seemed too... ordinary for him.

"Not exactly. But you haven't told me what was in your vision. It only seems fair that you share, too."

My eyes snapped open; I was suddenly alert. *Nope.* No way in hell was I telling Salem my vision. Gods, what was that about? Had there been... *spanking?* I'd sooner boil myself alive than tell him. I'd rip my arm right open again just to distract from this line of questioning.

Come up with a lie. "Parakeets," I blurted.

"Parakeets," he repeated.

I swallowed hard. "They terrify me. With their vaguely human voices, repeating words ad nauseam. It's just not right."

He arched an eyebrow. "Is there a reason you're blushing?"

"Look, I'm not going to tell my worst fears to the devil. Anyway, what do you care?"

"It's nothing more than a detached curiosity. It's just that I've never had shame, so I've never blushed."

The sunlight filtered through leaves above us and streamed over his wings. Every time I caught sight of them, of the fragmented bones sticking out, I had a sense of *wrongness*. My breath caught in my throat at the sight of them. Looking at the shattered wings felt like having a jagged knife scraping on the inside of my skull.

He deserved it, of course, for everything he'd done, and yet...

Maybe it was because his wings looked so delicate, but the sight of the blood spattering his feathers was too much. "Are you going to fix your wing?" I said, more irritated now.

He caught my gaze again, but ignored my question. Instead, he moved down to my leg and pressed another patch of moss against my thigh, just under my skirt. I winced as he lifted my leg a little to get the bandage around. It would have hurt a million times more if he hadn't already hit me with his healing magic.

He pressed his hand against my heart again, magic thrumming hot over my body. I breathed in the scent of him, the pomegranate and smoke. Something else there… a garden… a bone-deep, jagged sense of loss. Ragged emptiness, falling… A light snuffed out, spirit crushed into ash.

For just a moment, I almost felt like my heart was breaking.

"Falling," I whispered, not meaning to say it out loud.

Then he pulled his hand away abruptly. My eyes opened, and he stared at me.

"I didn't say anything," I added quickly. That was a worse lie than the parakeets.

After a moment, he said, "After a few hours of sleep, you'll be fine."

He rose and walked away from me, his wing practically hanging off him. *Wrong.*

I pulled my gaze away from him to survey my surroundings, wincing as I pushed up on my good arm.

It felt like a brief, peaceful respite here. Salem had laid me down on a mossy patch at a forest's edge. Sunlight pierced the branches, dappling the ground around me with dancing gold flecks. The sea breeze whispered over my skin, and leaves rustled above me.

As I watched Salem, I saw how he healed himself. Silvery-blue light flickered around his wings and feathers. His warrior's body beamed with light. His power rippled over me in waves, but he wasn't healing fast enough. His wing still looked ravaged.

Some strange instinct—like an invisible thread pulling

at my chest—forced me up onto my elbows, then onto my feet. A sharp tug yanked at my chest, drawing me closer to Salem.

I'd once read that a man who'd done too much cocaine found himself temporarily with a powerful sense of smell. Like an animal, he could tell when another person had been in the room or where they'd walked in the woods. He felt as if he were reclaiming something forgotten—a skill left dormant by evolution.

That was what this felt like—a buried knowledge coming alive again. A dim certainty that I could heal him, too, the way he'd healed me.

On my injured leg, I limped toward him. With his eyes closed, I had a clear look at his face, the sweep of dark eyelashes against his skin.

That tug on my chest compelled my hand to his sternum. His heart beat against my palm, steady and even. His eyes opened, and they burned with a bright blue as he looked down at me.

My sea magic rushed along my arm, pulsing into his body through my splayed fingers. It curled around him in wispy tendrils, twining with his magic.

I stared as his wings and feathers began to straighten a little. The music of our magic mingled together—his a deep rhythmic beat, and mine sad melodies that rose and fell.

"What do you want from all this?" I whispered, to myself more than to him.

His eyes focused, and he looked like he'd just snapped out of a spell. "To leave this place."

Now, his wings looked completely healed, the bones straight and feathers gleaming. His wings shimmered away.

"It's worked, right?" I asked. "Why, exactly, did that work? I've never done that before."

He studied my face, his brow furrowed. "Get some rest on the moss, Aenor. We need to move on from here soon."

24

SALEM

W hile Aenor slept, I patrolled the shore, staring out over the waves. I'd been here for hours in the sun, waiting for my sword to return to me. I'd lost Lightbringer in the sea, but she always found her way back.

Just like the sea was part of Aenor, my blade was a part of me. And while I waited for her to return, I felt her absence like a missing limb.

A stab of guilt shot through me. It was like I'd severed Aenor's soul when I took her magic away. I'd felt her loss when she'd healed me.

Guilt... What a ridiculous, useless feeling.

In any case, it wasn't as if she was blameless for her loss. She was my mate, that was all. A perverse twist of fate.

I glanced back at her where she slept soundly on the moss. I had an infuriating impulse to curl up next to her. In another life, she'd have been in my bed by now.

My chest tightened. Usually, I had a perverse compulsion to tell everyone everything. I laid out the wild beasts of my soul like a grotesque menagerie—here you see me burning humans for fun, and here are the broken hearts, and please don't miss the fact that I despise everyone alive. Look at my horror; feel revulsion.

It delighted me.

And yet with Aenor, I had to keep secrets—the secret that she was my mate.

I chafed against the constriction of it. I wanted to tell her everything all at once. I wanted to spill my secrets out like blood through the water.

The sea wind whipped over my body, howling.

Love was not part of my destiny, and it never could be. And here I was, prowling the shoreline like a wolf protecting his mate. Keeping her safe.

The waves lapped at my feet, warm and frothy, and a thrilling wind swelled over me. I tried to ignore the tiny blue will-o'-the-wisp buzzing around my head. That thing was a tiny spy, reporting back to my ancient enemies.

The sky darkened to ruddy hues as twilight arrived. Dipping lower, the sun seemed to grow larger over the horizon, yellow blending to harlot pink. As the lurid colors darkened to somber blue, the evening star gleamed—a jewel in the crown of the sky. That was where I belonged.

This was the time of day when my magic grew strongest, and when things crossed over from one world to another.

At last, a blue glint in the water heralded my sword's arrival. I felt the muscles in my chest unclench a little, and I rushed into the waves to get it. As soon as I had the iron hilt in my hand, power surged through my body, and I let out a long breath.

Unlike most fae, I wasn't hurt by iron. This iron came from the center of the evening star itself. The sword fit into my fist perfectly, and when I sheathed it again, I loosed a breath I'd been holding.

I'd lost my shirt when I bound Aenor's wounds, but I smoothed out my trousers, still damp from the sea. I hated looking disheveled.

When I reached Aenor, her eyes opened. I pulled my flask from my pocket to hand it to her.

She blinked. "Not really feeling like brandy right now."

"I filled it in a freshwater spring."

She sat up again, wincing a little, and took the flask from my hand. She drank from it deeply, then wiped the back of her hand across her mouth. "Thanks. How is it that you kept hold of your flask, but you lost your sword?"

"The sword always returns to me. The flask I have to keep a tighter grip on." I pulled it from her and drank from it deeply. When I looked back at her, I found that she'd fallen asleep again.

Her chest rose and fell slowly, her dark eyelashes sweeping across her skin. I wanted her to rest, but we had to move on.

I stood and crossed back to the shoreline. Something was nagging at the depths of my consciousness. Something that didn't quite seem right...

I scanned the churning sea as the sun lowered over the horizon.

Ah... there it was. It was almost imperceptible, the low, hissing sound around me, but it raised the hair on the back of my arms. I unsheathed Lightbringer, searching for the source of the noise. It grew louder behind me.

I whirled, catching a blue shimmer in the air. Something flitting around me, nearly transparent. Just a blue sheen floating on the breeze. Around me, the air grew cold, and webs of frost spread over my body.

This was how I'd felt around Beira, the Winter Witch, all those years ago. That icy hag wasn't here, was she?

Another hiss behind me, and I spun, gripping my sword.

Slowly, they materialized around me—swords drawn. They were muscular fae in scaled armor, eyes murky like the sea. Six of them stood before me, wearing the Merrow's symbol—the trident encircled by a snake. "We won't let you unleash the Fomorians. We won't let you burn the world."

My heart pounded like a war drum. I was ready to kill them all. But when I swung for one of them, he disappeared. My sword cut through shimmering air.

I conjured my magic, searing the air around me with heat. Smoke wrapped me in darkness.

My lip curled. Phantom fae always got on my nerves— denying you that delicious thrill of a blade carving through bone and flesh.

The fae materialized again, lunging for me with his sword.

I moved faster, whirling and ducking as the warriors attacked through the smoke. Another hot pulse of my magic blazed down my sword. The air smelled singed—burned cloth and flesh.

That was interesting. Even if I couldn't cut them with a blade, they seemed vulnerable to fire.

But they outnumbered me, and one of them caught me in the back with his blade.

Anger started rising in me. All this to protect what the Merrow did—a sin.

I spun, moving faster now, my burning blade searing their flesh a little before they flickered away again. Sweat dripped down their faces as I burned the air.

Even so, there were more of them now, bodies flickering into existence around me.

My wings shot out behind me, but the fae had penned me in too close for me to lift off. One of their swords came down into my wing, and pain screamed through my wing bones and my shoulder.

Then—as if this situation weren't bad enough—a shimmer of blue light darted toward Aenor. Wrath coiled around me, hot as the flames of hell. It burned away my sense of panic.

I'd protect her. I'd bathe the world in flames just to save her.

Fire, my oldest companion...

I spread my arms, and furious magic electrified my body. Flames spread from my chest—like the old days in the caves of Gehenna. More assassins kept flickering into the air around me, but I'd burn them all to ash.

Now, at last, I saw the fear in their faces as they burned. They trembled before me like I was a god.

25

AENOR

I woke to the sound of screaming and the scent of burning flesh. Fear slammed into me. Gods below, was it all over? Were the Fomorians burning it all already?

But just as I was clearing the fog of sleep from my eyes, someone lunged for me from the shadows. Fear hit me like a fist as the sea fae pressed a wet, icy blade to my throat. His green hair snaked around his head like he was underwater, and his pale body gleamed in the moonlight. He wore the symbol of the Merrow.

Smoke filled the air. In contrast to the chill of the blade, the air around us felt far too hot.

Even with his weapon at my throat, I could kill him, I thought. I could desiccate him into a withered husk. I glanced over his shoulder, where I caught a glimpse of Salem fighting others like him. Flames engulfed them, and the heat was spreading even here.

Except—he was an agent of the Merrow. And that meant I needed him.

"I'm on your side," I whispered hastily. "I tried to get a message to the Merrow. I need his help."

"The Merrow has been imprisoned. He will not be able to help you."

My blood turned to ice. "But I need him. It's what the book said. The Merrow can trap him."

The sea fae shook his head. "He can't trap him anymore. Anyway, you don't need Salem trapped. It just makes things harder for you, not impossible."

"Who are you?"

"An agent of the Merrow. We're secretly working for him while he's imprisoned in Mag Mell. Now tell me—do you plan to kill Salem or are you helping him?"

"I need the sea glass," I whispered. "Can you find it? I thought the Merrow would have it." I whispered.

"I haven't been able to speak to him since he was imprisoned."

Son of a gun. My stomach twisted at this news. "Fine, so you need to find the sea glass. Bring it to me. Then I can kill Salem." The words *I can kill Salem* now felt wrong to me. Sickening, almost.

The fae nodded once, lessening the pressure on the blade just a little. "I'll try to bring it to you. Make your way to Mag Mell, and we'll get the sea glass to you." Slowly, he pulled the blade from my neck.

"Who is she?" I asked. "The woman in the soul cage?"

He opened his mouth, but before he could answer, his body ignited in flames, hair blazing like a torch. His body flickered away, but not before I heard his agonized screams.

My stomach dropped. And there went my best chance to get the sea glass.

What the hells was I supposed to do now?

The air heated around me, so hot and dry it felt like I'd been thrown into the sun. *Salem will kill us all.*

My throat tightened at the sight of flames rising tall

above him, a cathedral of fire. Dark wings swept down his back, and short horns jutted from his shoulder blades. The fire had ignited his feathers, but that didn't seem to bother him. His eyes were locked only on me.

I glanced at his sword, and for a moment I thought he was going to use it on me. Instead, he held out a hand to me like he was my savior. A savior from the mouth of hell.

"What happened?" I asked, my voice hoarse.

As if I didn't already know.

"The Merrow send his soldiers to kill us." He cocked his head. "Or perhaps to kill me and save you. In any case, I had to burn them, of course. I'll burn anyone who gets in my way."

A hint of steel undercut his velvety tone, and a threat trembled over my skin. Had me heard me promising to kill him?

I held his gaze steadily. "Well, I guess I have to put out the flames."

I took a step back from him, finding the heat unbearable. Cold water slid down my body as my magic surged. I tasted salt on my lips and called to the sea.

Droplets of ocean water formed in the air, the sea spume spraying over my body. The water started falling harder and harder, a torrent of ocean, dousing the flames. A swell of frigid sea wind swept over me.

As my magic built in strength, so did the intensity of the sensations around me. The sound of the rain on the forest floor was like hammers hitting metal, cold raindrops like pellets of ice. When I opened my eyes, I saw the moon blazing white.

So much beauty, but too bright, too loud. A heartbreakingly beautiful man stood before me, but he had to die.

My emotions, too, were spiraling wildly. I stared at

Salem as his wings disappeared, the rain sliding down his skin. My mind flickered with that jagged sense of loss I'd felt when touching his chest. As I glanced at his heart, a bottom-less well of sadness opened in my chest. That was where I was supposed to put the sea glass—right into his aorta.

I reached up to touch his face. His skin felt so hot, his eyes bright as stars.

When Salem touched my waist, the intensity of my emotions began to calm. The seawater was surging around us now, rushing in from the shoreline. It lapped at my legs.

Salem leaned down, whispering in my ear among the torrent of rain. "You need to channel the magic. Root your-self to the earth. Feel where your feet are."

I took a deep breath, focusing on my feet. In my mind's eye, I could see my magic as bright sea-green light. I imag-ined it moving slowly up and down my legs, spreading into the earth. The soil absorbed some of its power beneath where I stood, and I sighed with relief.

I found myself leaning against Salem's chest, drawn to his warmth. The rain started to fall lighter now.

But Salem's words sliced through my sense of calm.

"Get the boat ready. Command it to sail to Mag Mell. We're leaving."

You're leaving for your death, friend.

26

SALEM

I sat in the boat Aenor had conjured. Moonlight glistened over her wet blue hair, and the sea spray dampened us both.

At this point, it seemed insane that I'd taken her at her word. I'd asked if she was taking me to the Merrow. I knew she was bringing me to Mag Mell, because I'd heard her command the boat.

What I hadn't asked explicitly was if she planned to help me get the soul cage back. Or if she planned to kill me.

Somehow I'd started feeling like we were on the same side, like we were working together.

But I'd heard what she said to that sea fae. *I am the only one who can kill him.*

She didn't know she was my mate, though, did she?

In any case, I had to kill her before she killed me. As soon as she got close to my heart with a blade, I'd end her life.

For the first time in millennia, I had a flame burning in my chest, and killing Aenor would smother it. But what choice did I have?

There were greater destinies in this world than mating like animals.

When I thought of ending her life, coldness spread through my body. Then a feeling like I was plummeting faster than a meteor, the wind whipping at my body. Unmoored and lost to the darkness.

I gripped the side of the boat, the sun rays strangely cold on my chest.

Aenor's stomach rumbled, and my muscles tensed with a compulsive need to feed her. We hadn't eaten since this morning. She must be as starving as I was.

She flashed me a sad smile. "If you don't burn the world down, I'm going to learn to make homemade cake pops."

"Cake pops," I repeated. Even hungry as I was, they sounded dreadful.

"It's like a lollipop, but made of cake. A little stick with a cake ball coated in frosting."

Interesting. "Perhaps I want to eat your cake pops," I said carefully.

She smiled, radiant. "All you have to do is not light the world on fire. I'll make chocolate, lemon, and red velvet. With sprinkles."

I didn't even like sweets, but this sounded oddly tempting.

Aenor dipped her fingers in the water, her body glowing with sea magic. "Instead of destroying the world, Salem, you could take back your kingdom. I'd even help you."

Well, this was a surprising turn of events. "You'd help me take over Mag Mell? And what would *Lyr* say about that?"

"I really don't give a crap."

The violence of this statement both surprised and pleased me. "Is that right?"

She looked out at the sea again, leaning on her elbow.

"Lyr and I aren't exactly speaking. He tried to take my magic from me with some kind of binding collar."

White-hot anger erupted in my chest. I'd delight in lighting his fortress on fire. "He tried to do *what?*"

She shot me a sharp look. "I don't know why I'm telling you this. Forget I said anything." She sighed. "Let's get back to taking over your kingdom. You could be happy again. You could get a palace. You can live out your debauched fantasies. Make it more debauched, even. Nymph wrestling. Naked roller derby. Rivers of brandy and harems of mermaid concubines. I don't even want to know how mermaids have sex, but I'm sure you wouldn't get bored."

I desired only one person in my bed from now until eternity, and I had to kill her. "Are you trying to tempt me from my true path? I do believe temptation is traditionally my job, Aenor. But please, keep describing this paradise. I'm most interested in your naked roller-skating fantasy."

My desire to see her unclothed was nearly overwhelming. She would make me insane if I spent too much time around her.

In the darkness, her eyes gleamed bright. "So who is this woman you want to save? I want to know."

Oh, you beautiful little liar. We aren't going to rescue anyone, since you're going to assassinate me. I am going to rescue her, and I don't know what fate holds for you.

Might as well tell her the truth now. What difference did it make?

She'd probably be dead soon.

Cold ash in my chest, plunging to earth... Falling so fast through the cold, the light burns out on the way down...

"Her name is Shahar," I said quietly. "We were twins in the heavens. Before the fall, she was goddess of the dawn. Some called her the morning star. In dawn, she was most powerful, when she beamed over the earth. I was god of the dusk. The evening star. Both of our souls were tied to one celestial body that showed up in the morning and at night. One star, imbued with the souls of two gods. In the heavens, Shahar and I were bound to each other. Part of each other. Now, that celestial body hangs in the heavens, devoid of a soul. Shahar and I have been severed from each other, our light ripped from us." What I wouldn't give for my brandy right now. "When I fell to earth, it was like my soul burned out on the way down."

She nodded. "The pain from losing your magic. It sounds familiar."

"Well, now you will learn why it happened to you, Aenor. Do you remember when I told you about Gehenna, how I watched as sacrifices burned around me? I had become the beast everyone believed me to be. I wanted to kill everything that moved. I seduced every female who caught my eye, just to break their hearts and leave them mad. Shahar was the one who pulled me out of that hell. She made me civilized again. She had to keep me locked in her home for years, but slowly I learned to become civilized again, to control my impulses. Slowly, she helped me smother the beast inside me. He's still there, but he's been quiet for centuries."

Aenor's brow furrowed. "And the Fomorians?"

"To my knowledge, she had no interest in the Fomorians. It would be fun to watch the world burn, I suppose, but it's not high on my list of priorities."

"To your *knowledge*..." she repeated, like this was an interrogation in a courtroom.

"I know her as well as you can know anyone. We've always been linked, but she got the best parts of our twinned souls, while I got the worst. She never hurt anyone.

I'll tell you what she did: she worshipped the dawn every morning. She swam in the sea and baked her own bread. She played a flute, and she took in cats who were sick or injured. She liked to thread wildflowers into her hair and sing lullabies to her pets. She sewed Jacobean ruffs for her cats and fashioned them fancy beds with lace. That's who you drowned. Not a monster."

I'm the monster. I'm the one you should have drowned, Aenor.

"When you sank her beneath the waves," I continued, anger rising, "did you know she had four children, or that she drank brandy with me in the evenings so we could watch the twilight fall over the sea?"

Aenor stared at me, the wind whipping her hair into her face. She looked positively resolute. "I'm sorry about your sister. But I've seen the visions. And before I killed that Fomorian, he literally said, *Salem, the evening star, the fallen king of Mag Mell. He will set us free.* It was *very* specific."

Interesting. "You killed one?"

"Yes. I know, nobody believes they exist."

"I believe what you say. You killed a Fomorian. But do you really think I'd leave my sister trapped in the sea because of some wretched fire fae? Do you think I'd abandon her for a kingdom? I thought she was dead." Guilt coiled through me. "I think your mother drowned her so she could use Shahar's power for herself. The rest was a lie."

She shook her head. "We didn't use her magic."

"Do you know that?" My voice was a cold blade.

"No," she admitted. "The soul cage drained her power from her body, and her magic now lights up the water outside the cage. Maybe her magic stopped the world from burning. Maybe it helped to keep the Fomorians trapped."

"When I arrived at Ys to destroy it, I thought she was dead. What I didn't know was that you'd trapped her in the darkness, under a thousand tons of water, alone and in pain."

Aenor shifted in her seat, her eyes laser-focused on me. "So what changed? How did you learn the truth?"

"That hardly seems like the most pressing question."

"But it is. Someone passed this information on to you. Someone has an agenda."

I shrugged. "I received the information in the form of an anonymous message. Whatever the agenda is, it doesn't matter to me."

She hugged herself. "When you arrived in Ys to destroy it, and you killed my mother, why didn't you kill me? You knew I was part of it."

That compulsion again, to tell her the truth. "I didn't want to kill you, that's why. Your mother lied to you, Aenor. Shahar wasn't going to burn the world down. If anything, you put the world in more danger when you took her away from me. I am the real threat, and she once tempered my rages." The night wind whipped over my skin. "When we get to Mag Mell, Aenor, I want you to stay close to me. You'll be with me until the very end. Until we find Shahar in the depths. Only then will I release you."

I couldn't allow her to conspire with the Merrow's agents, to find whatever weapon she needed to kill me. She sighed with frustration. How *sad* she must be that I was making it harder for her to rip my heart from my chest. A true tragedy for my beloved.

"Give me a chance to show you what will happen," she said, desperate now. "I'll show you what will happen if you get this soul cage out of the ocean."

She still thought she could stop me, even after what I'd told her.

I leaned forward, my hands on my knees, and felt myself

falling again, plunging through dark space. "Here is what you need to understand about me, Aenor. The world can burn, for all I care. I'll release the Fomorians if that's what it takes. I'm going to get Shahar, and I don't care at all if everything else turns to ash. Even you."

The lie tasted bitter on my tongue.

27

AENOR

We drifted under the moonlight, bobbing on the waves. With the stars beaming above us, I'd fallen asleep in the rocking boat.

I woke to a feeling of warmth, of safety. Bliss hummed along my skin. I sighed, with the slowly dawning realization that masculine arms encircled me, and my head lay against a powerful male chest. For one pure moment, a sense of total protection wrapped around me like a cloud. A sense of completion pounded in my blood in time to his heartbeat...

Then I realized *whom* I was leaning against, and my chest flushed.

"Not today, Satan," I muttered. I sat bolt upright, glowering at him. "Were your arms around me?"

He leaned back on his elbows against the side of the boat, the wind ruffling his hair. "Your teeth were chattering. It was ruining the peace. And do you have any idea how loud you snore? Aenor Dahut, Scourge of the Silence, Ruiner of Peace."

I blinked, shocked at how much time had passed.

The first rays of dawn light began to spread over the sea,

a dazzling liquid amber on the ripples. Winding wisps of fog curled around us.

"I slept all night?" When I dipped my fingertips in the water, I felt disturbed by its warmth.

"We're almost there," he said.

I turned, catching a glimpse of Mag Mell. It wasn't exactly what I'd imagined. Instead of an untouched paradise, it was a city built on a rocky hill, surrounded by seawalls. At the hill's peak, a castle towered above the sea. Morning light bathed its stony spires in gold. And between the castle and the seawalls grew a wild-looking forest of oaks and rowan trees.

Shimmering magic streamed up to the skies from above the city walls—transparent gold.

"What's that?" I asked. "The magic around the city?"

"Well, that's to keep me out, given that I can fly. The city gates are guarded. But before I left the kingdom, I hid a key to the city in case I ever needed to return. There are wards there to stop anyone like me from flying over the kingdom, but with the key, I can destroy them."

"And how do we get past the guards?"

He looked at me like I was an idiot. "We kill them and throw their bodies in the water."

"Of course." *Or* I got to them first and begged them to take me to the Merrow in his prison.

"It hasn't changed much," said Salem quietly. "At least, I think it hasn't. I'll inspect it more closely."

I needed to get away from him, to hunt for the Merrow on my own. Did the old sorcerer have more assassins working for him in Mag Mell, where he was imprisoned?

I cleared my throat. "Are you sure you still need me? We both know the Merrow is on this island somewhere. You just need to find him and beat the truth out of him."

He seemed to hesitate then, uncharacteristically unsure of himself. "As I said, you're staying with me until it's all over."

"I'll do my best to get you to her." *Lie, lie, lie.*

It was my job to kill the bad guys. I cut out their hearts, nailed them to my wall. Salem was the worst of them all.

So why did the thought of killing him make me want to vomit?

Maybe it was that most of them hadn't sat me down to tell me their life story, or about how they'd loved their sisters, or the cats with lace collars. Nor had I met their pets, for crying out loud.

I'd gone into this thinking he wanted to burn the world down for fun, but now it seemed that wasn't a part of his plan. It was a side effect, maybe of freeing the sister he loved.

The mist thickened around us.

"We can't go any further in the boat," he said. "They'll sound the alarm if they see an unfamiliar vessel pulling up."

"So we swim underwater," I said. "But where to?"

"You swim underwater. I'm going to fly around the perimeter once or twice to see what I can see. I'll circle the island first, getting an idea of the layout." He pointed at wooden docks jutting from the seawalls. Colorful silk sails festooned the masts around the port. "Meet me by that gate. You can wait under the dock until I arrive so the guards don't see you. I'll handle them."

"And once we kill the guards?"

"We will be in the Forest of Wandering Souls. It's a disorienting place. When you find yourself confused, focus on your feet on the earth. Just like you did before."

"So that's it? It's just disorienting?"

"Unless times have changed, a *baobhan sith* patrols the

forest. While you're confused, she will hunt you down and rip you apart with her iron claws. So try not to let that happen."

"I'll do my best to avoid her. They're fae witches, right? But am I right in thinking the *baobhan sith* makes you dance until you've gone insane?"

"Yes." He flashed me a wry smile. "Then she slashes your chest open with her talons and drinks your blood from your entrails." His calm, velvety voice belied the horror of what he was telling me. "So try to keep your wits about you. Once we get past the Forest of Wandering souls, we'll go through the proper city gates and try to find the Merrow."

I'd have to go through with the charade of searching for the Merrow when I knew exactly where he was—in the castle dungeon.

Somehow, I had to break free from Salem. I had to get a message to the Merrow in his dungeon, which meant finding my way to the castle alone.

"Can you still hear the Merrow's music?"

I dipped my fingers in the water and felt his song vibrating through the waves. Odd, considering he was supposed to be in a dungeon. How was his music traveling through the water? "Yes. I can hear it."

"Good." Salem stood in the boat, the morning light sculpting his muscled chest.

Then his dark wings erupted behind him—black and dusky violet, streaked with gold. My breath caught at the sight of them.

His magic whispered over me as his wings beat the air. He lifted up from the boat, soaring into the misty skies above us.

For a moment, I watched him fly. Then I leapt off the

boat, plunging deep under the water. As I swam, the sea's warmth heated my skin. Far too hot for the Atlantic.

They were coming, the Fomorians. It was like they were gathering near here, ready to break free.

I whirled in the water, trying to find the source of heat. It seemed to be coming from the seafloor. I dove deeper.

As I swam closer to the seafloor, I felt its heat. The ocean was warming from the floor upward, and little fissures had opened in the sand. A faint sheen of red magic shone through. Gods, it was boiling down here.

They'd gathered here, in this part of the sea, and death whispered around me. They knew Salem would set them free.

My blood pounded in my body, a deep war drum. The dead Fomorian's words rang in my mind.

Salem, evening star, Fallen King of Mag Mell, will set us free.

The glowing red light from a crack in the seafloor beamed out over everything around it. At the bottom, I reached for the rocks. When I stroked my fingertips over them, I winced as the heat burned me. The stench of death curled upward as life began to rot and die around me. Under the water, I took in the withered sea life. Muscles and cockles around me were dying in a hot grave.

Gods below.

Dread bloomed in my chest as I started to head up higher. My skin flushed in the warm sea, pulse racing. I kicked my feet, my body overheating. I was moving fast for the shore, trying to get away from the heat.

At last, by the port, I breached the surface under a dock. Was there any chance I could appeal to the guards to help me? From one end of the old wooden dock, I pulled myself up, peering over the surface's edge.

A row of guards patrolled the gate, dressed in red

uniforms. They carried spears that gleamed with silvery magic, and their armor gleamed in the morning light.

I glanced up at the sky, but I didn't see Salem yet.

Adrenaline sparked in my nerves, my chest rising and falling fast. Maybe I could get to them fast, ask them the quickest route to the castle before Salem arrived.

I hoisted myself up, body shaking. One of the guards turned toward me, his pale hair caught in the sea wind. He glared at me, gripping his spear. Then his expression changed as he took in my wet clothes.

I held up my hands, showing him I was unarmed, and took a step closer.

I *really* didn't like the way the guards were leering, but I remembered what Salem had said. This was a hedonist's paradise. They probably weren't used to seeing women in clothes and probably assumed we had only one purpose.

The man at the front took a step closer, biting his lip. "We'll need you to take off those clothes, so we can inspect you fully for weapons."

"Strip for us, now," said another. "Give us a good look."

"I'm not here for that." Icy magic tingled down my arms, and my fingers twitched with violent impulses. Aaah... I'd forgotten how my magic felt when I wanted to rip someone's head off. It was truly electrifying.

Except I couldn't kill him when I needed information from him.

"Just tell me how to get to the castle before I kill you all," I snapped.

The guard smiled, eyes still on my breasts. "Strip, or tell me the password."

"The password?"

Another step closer, inches from me now. "If you belong here, you'd know it."

In the depths of my mind, I pictured him drowning. "Is it... 'password'? But with an *at* symbol for the a? I have no idea. Are the esses dollar signs? Did you hear the part about how I can kill you?"

He stepped closer, grabbing me by the collar of my shirt like he was going to pull it off. "Must you keep talking, little girl?"

"Is the password 'get the hell off me or I'll drop the sea on your head'?" I snarled.

Lesson learned. Don't go to the guards for help.

The guard pulled me closer, pressing his groin against me. And that was all I needed for my sea magic to electrify my body.

I brought my knee up hard into his crotch, and he doubled over. I swung for him, punching him hard in the jaw so hard that I cracked the bone. The other guards pulled their swords.

I summoned a sword of ice. Then I slammed it into the neck of the man who'd grabbed me.

A wave of violence crashed through me, and I wanted to bring the sea down hard on these men, except an oncoming tsunami was likely to draw a bit of attention.

Maybe I should try to avoid an all-out war.

As my sword clashed with another guard's, I caught a glimpse of more soldiers pouring through the gate.

I moved fast as a storm wind and pivoted to strike another. I ducked as a blade came for my head, then whirled—low to the ground, slamming my blade into a guard's legs.

Euphoria rippled through me. I wanted to drown them all, crush them into the ocean floor...

Then a burst of silky magic washed over me, thrumming over my skin. Calming my rage. When I looked up, I saw him. Salem swooped down from the heavens, his sword blazing with pale fire, wings outstretched. He swung his sword, severing a guard in half at the waist. He touched down, and the blade arced through another—carving through flesh and bone soundlessly.

My own sword was a whirlwind of ice and blood. I pivoted fast, fury snapping through my nerve endings. One by one, the dead guards fell to the ground, blood pooling over the stones.

Breathing deeply, I channeled my magic to gain control, and it flowed up and down my legs, spreading through the wood of the dock. Slowly, the magical charge simmered down until I felt in control again. I caught my breath, and the sword of ice shimmered away.

Salem stared at the guards' bodies, blood dripping from his sword. "Perhaps I shouldn't have ruined their uniforms. They might have come in handy." He sheathed his sword. "What exactly happened? How did you end up fighting them before I got here?"

I took a deep breath. "They spotted me under the dock," I lied. "Thought they could take advantage of a helpless little morgen."

"I saw you from above. I saw you approach them. In any case, they deserved to die. They work for the king who usurped my crown." His eyes burned into me. "Traitors deserve death, don't you think? Betrayal is perhaps the worst of sins. Those who promise something to one person, while secretly conspiring against him."

He knew. He definitely knew.

And he was just biding his time before he killed me.

28

SALEM

I incinerated the bodies in moments, bones and flesh turning to ash. The curling black smoke could draw a bit of attention, I supposed, from other guards. Still less attention than a dozen guards' bodies. Within moments, there was nothing left of the patrol but a few piles of ash.

I glanced up at the gateway to my kingdom—a stone gate engraved with images of the stars. And between the stars, crows. My usurper had added the bloody crows.

From what I could tell after my flight around the city walls, Tethra still ruled here. I was half tempted to raze this whole place, but that wouldn't get me to the Merrow.

I glanced at Aenor, her body still sparkling with her magic. She looked the most enchanting when she used her power.

The look she shot me, however, was pure hatred. It was quite amazing, really, that someone could despise their fated mate that much.

Then again, inspiring loathing was my greatest power.

Would it have been different if she'd been with me when

I ruled here, or would the emptiness within still have torn me in two?

No point in dwelling on what might have been.

"What did you see?" she asked.

"What I saw is that the kingdom has fallen into ruin. Monsters, crumbling buildings, wild fae dancing around a fire. Beyond that, I couldn't see much without flying directly over the island." I frowned. "You heard him through the water?"

She nodded. "Yes. Are there rivers? A moat?"

"Several rivers, streams, a moat that floods the lower level of the castle."

She nodded, then looked up at the dark castle that loomed over the island. She was thinking something she wasn't sharing.

Was the Merrow, perhaps, in the palace? I'd find out soon enough. I could fly right into one of the upper towers, with Aenor's legs wrapped around me, her hips tight against mine...

In any case, we'd bypass all the security.

I scrubbed a hand over my jaw. Before they'd exiled me, I'd hidden a key in a hollow oak in the winter forest. It had the power to burn down the wards. But that was millennia ago, and the tree would have long since crumbled into the earth.

"Let's go." I started walking, and Aenor walked silently by my side.

I thought I could still remember where the tree had grown. If I were lucky, the earth would have swallowed the key in exactly the same spot. I should be able to feel its magical vibrations, I thought.

I glanced at Aenor, and a blade of longing pierced my heart.

I shouldn't be longing for things on earth when I'd be rising to the heavens so soon.

We crossed into a forest of dark, jagged trees jutting from the snow. Spare, bony branches clawed the sky above us.

Rays of sunlight streamed through the gnarled branches, honeyed chinks of light on the wintry landscape. A few fragments of ruined buildings stood between the trees, encased in ice.

A dirt path meandered through the snow, but all around us it was winter. As we walked deeper into the thickly wooded forest, the boughs above us grew thicker, blocking out more light. It was as if night had fallen all around us. Now, I couldn't see anything of the city gates or my castle that loomed above us.

Once, there'd been three *baobhan sith* here, but only one remained.

At least, I thought only one remained...

What did I really know about this place anymore? The *baobhan sith* and I had something of a history—witches, prone to cursing as well as tearing people to bits. In fact, it was a *baobhan sith* who'd forced me from this kingdom. The Winter Witch.

I'd gotten my revenge on her, at least.

Perhaps I'd light the remaining witch on fire.

The snowfall stuck in Aenor's eyelashes and landed on her pink cheeks, on the tip of her nose. I wanted to warm her up, except she didn't seem to mind the cold, even in her wet clothes.

And there she was, distracting me again.

As soon as the thought had formed in my mind, an ice-cold talon raked down my spine—a witch's warning.

I whirled, unsheathing my sword. Lightbringer flickered

with blue magic, but the *baobhan sith* had already disappeared.

"What was that?" Aenor whispered. "Was that the witch?"

"I think so," I said quietly.

As soon as the words were out of my mouth, the forest started to darken even further, shadows claiming the trees like spilled ink. Through the darkness, I caught a glimpse of white hair flashing, long, dark nails. Then she was gone again.

My heart leapt a little when Aenor took a step closer to me. Protectiveness surged.

Gripping my sword, I scanned the dark trees for signs of the witch. The snow fell harder in a wild vortex around us. Already, we'd gone off the path somehow. When had we gone off the bloody path?

Gods, it was already harder to focus. The *baobhan sith* had grown more powerful over the years. Or perhaps it was easier to manipulate my desire when my mate was only inches from me.

You see, the Ollephest gave you an image of your worst fears.

But the *baobhan sith* gave you a vision of your greatest desires. They played you like an instrument, compelling you to dance and sing, dreaming of all the things you wanted. Then they feasted on your organs.

They were bottomless pits of desire and loneliness. I supposed I had that in common with her, at least.

And yet even as I warned myself to focus, already my mind was spinning with visions of Aenor straddling my lap, running her fingers through my hair. Her eyes shone with desire, worship as she looked at me.

I clenched my jaw, trying to focus through the haze of

pleasure. I had to keep her safe, and that meant keeping my wits about me...

But she was crossing to me, naked, across a stone floor, her blue hair loose over her shoulders, eyes shining. She lay on a bed before me, smiling, legs spread...

This was what would have been if I'd met her all those years ago, before I'd become what I was now.

She can't be mine for good. I can't love her. I can't love, not even my mate.

Still, even if I couldn't love, I could protect her from this monster. I tightened my grip on Lightbringer. Then a flicker of pale movement caught my eye, and I swung.

It cut through nothing but air.

I cursed myself. Had I even known what I was swinging for? I could hardly see. What if I hit Aenor? Gods, was there anything worse than killing your own mate?

I shook my head, trying to clear it until I had my bearings. I stood in the dark forest again.

Killing your own mate... I'd been thinking of doing just that, hadn't I? That was actually my plan.

Ending my own mate's life.

Whenever I thought of it, I felt myself plunging through the heavens, the fire in my heart snuffing out. *Lost.*

"Aenor." My voice sounded husky, pleading. Unfamiliar. "Stay close."

Another glimpse of the witch between the trunks, then a blazing vision of ecstasy beguiled my thoughts. Aenor was in my lap now, her legs wrapped around my waist, kissing my neck with languid strokes of her tongue. I could feel her body's need for me, and I wanted to make her shudder with pleasure.

With an iron will, I forced the dream from my mind. Cold, dead trees jutting from the snow, a squall of sparkling flakes whirling around me. And Aenor standing in the center of it all. She'd conjured her icy sword, but she looked lost, consumed by visions herself.

Was she thinking of me?

Whatever the case, I had to keep her safe from this vile monster.

Fire roared in my chest, melting away my dreams.

Now, I could see the clear path wending through the forest. But when I grabbed Aenor's hand to pull her along, a new vision clouded in my mind. It was the island of Ys before I'd sunk it.

A little girl with blue hair stood on a seaside cliff, surrounded by wildflowers of gold and periwinkle. The sun streamed over the landscape, lemon yellow, glinting off the water. The girl laughed, flicking her hands above the sea. At her command, the waves roared higher, and the bells of Ys tolled.

Aenor's desires were seeping into my own mind as I held her hand.

The little girl turned to see a woman wearing a yellowed wedding dress, silver-blue hair threaded with narcissus flowers and seashells. Aenor's mother.

She crossed to Aenor and stroked her hair, pulling her close. Her green eyes shone with pride.

I dropped Aenor's hand, clearing my mind of the vision. I spun, looking for the *baobhan sith*.

"Aenor," I whispered. "Stay with me. Use your loathing of me to forget everything happy."

She cut me a sharp look that told me she was back with me and gripped her ice sword.

I'd seen her vision of perfect happiness—her mother's pride. The same mother I'd killed. No wonder she despised me down to my bones.

But the saddest part of her vision was that I didn't think anything like that had ever happened. In real life, Queen Malgven wore a dress stained with old blood. It had been clean in the vision. And Queen Malgven wasn't proud of her daughter, was she? She hadn't trusted her daughter enough to keep her sober. She'd gotten Aenor drunk to drown Shahar, hiding the truth from her.

Aenor's breath clouded around her head, eyes alert. "There's more than one *baobhan sith*."

Flaming gods.

She was more alert that I was. And now, I saw what she meant—the flashes of white between he trees, moving like ghosts. Their skin so pale it had a blue sheen. No wonder they had the power to confuse me so easily.

As my eyes sharpened, I caught the white, ragged cloth hanging off their bony bodies, trailing in the wintry winds. So many of them...

My impulse was to burn everything around me—but that would mean Aenor, too. She was entirely too flammable. If I used my fire, I'd have to be very careful.

Icy webs of frost spread in my chest. The witch had *spawned*. And if I couldn't keep a clear head, they'd drain Aenor's blood while I dreamt.

29

AENOR

I'd just been back in Ys, looking at Mama. And now I was in a creepy-ass forest, surrounded by winter witches. It looked like a dozen Beiras out there, flickering through the trees, white hair streaming in the wind. The snow crunched under my bare feet.

Sadly, in the hierarchy of situations in which my ice powers were helpful, fighting snow witches was somewhere at the bottom.

Gods, I was so close. I wondered if the Merrow could see me with his scrying powers from the dungeon. Did he know I was coming for him?

Footfalls in the snow made my heart race, and I turned to see one of the witches. My heart skipped a beat. She cocked her head, blue lips twitching, soundless. She blinked, three bloodshot eyes, and reached for me. Her body glowed with pearly light.

I swung my ice sword at her, but it shattered against her body, ice chips sparking in the dim light. The witch's grin split her pale face, exposing her long teeth. Death shone in her eyes.

I whirled again, and another witch was upon me. Panic climbed up my throat.

But when someone stroked a dark claw down my arm, euphoria sang through my body. All my fear disappeared. My heart beat hard, a drumbeat luring me to move. The witches faded away around me, until there was nothing left but starlight beaming onto the snow.

Never put your faith in a man. Mama's voice rang in my head. *They'll break your heart every time.*

But there was music now. I could dance, and I didn't need to worry about men. Didn't need to worry about Mama, or the bloodstain on her dress, or how her eyes bulged when she died. Didn't need to worry about the beautiful man I had to kill.

Joy coursed through my veins, the music of the spheres, and I could dance and dance. My feet pounded the snow, harder and harder. Frantic now, whirling, snow spinning around me. So fast...

My feet slammed the cold earth, the euphoria faded, and I didn't feel a thing now. Numb through my body.

It was just me and the winter dance here, me and the wild melody of the witch music. Thoughts of sea glass and burning cities faded to icy stillness.

Music screeched in my ears, and I threw my arms above my head as I spun. My feet kicked up snowflakes. I whirled and whirled to the beat of the music, until the strength started draining from my body.

Now, the music seemed too loud, my feet cold in the snow. Gods, I wanted to stop dancing.

Why wouldn't my feet stop moving? A sense of fatigue ate through the numbness, muscles shrieking. As I twirled, my hair whipped around my head, into my eyes. Sharp cold spread through my fingers, my toes, like they were blackening with ice.

At least I couldn't feel my heart breaking anymore.

Someone was shouting my name, that deep, velvety voice undercut with steel. I smelled him—sweet and dark. I felt the chasm in his chest as he called to me.

Salem.

The steady beat of his music replaced the wildness of the witch song. Slowly, the urge to dance started to fade in me, and my limbs began to pump with warm blood again. My feet stilled on the cold ground. I caught my breath, feeling like my magic had burned out. I'd need time to recharge before I had my strength again.

As my vision cleared. I spotted the witches again in the distance, between the trees. A few swooped above me, ragged vultures above the branches.

They could fly?

My heart thundered. On the ground, they'd surrounded Salem, shrieking as they ripped into him with their claws, pulling his wings apart, blood and feathers raining around them.

No.

A wild flame of protectiveness flickered in me... odd. Considering I planned to kill him.

I broke into a run, ignoring the voice in the back of my head that whispered, *Maybe you should let the witches take him down. Maybe you should get the sea glass while they rip him to pieces.* A primal instinct propelled me forward; I was desperate to rip him free.

As I ran, Salem roared and swung his sword, severing two of the witches in half. Blue fire flickered over their bodies. But they didn't seem to be dead, given that they were still screaming.

Then, from behind, a powerful force slammed into me, knocking me face-first into the snow. Before I could right myself, iron claws jammed into my side, and I grunted at the pain. Iron was poison to most fae, and I could feel the toxins sliding through my body.

I slammed my elbow backward, hitting the witch's jaw.

What was left of my magic started rising in my body. I bashed her again with my elbows—this time in her ribs—and broke free. Overhead, a witch was swooping for me.

She might be scary, but so was I. Aenor, Scourge of the Wicked, Flayer of Skins.

I ducked, avoiding a swipe of oncoming claws. When she swooped around again, I grabbed her from below, hands around her scrawny neck. Maybe my ice magic wasn't helpful against a snow witch, but my power was recharging now.

I had strength on my side. Snarling, I crushed her throat. When her three eyes bulged wide, I gripped her head in both of my hands. I snapped her neck. The crack of bone echoed off the trees, louder than it should have been.

It sent all the other witches cawing like crows, running for me, tattered white rags trailing behind. Their movements were so quiet...

My body charged with magic. As the first witch reached me, I slammed a fist into her face.

But there were so many of them, on me like a mob, dragging me down. I shouted for Salem as they pinned me, iron claws digging into my arms. The power of the sea crashed through me, ready to erupt. One of the witches knelt on my chest, spittle flying from her lips. I punched her hard, cracking her skull. She slid off me.

Scrambling to my feet, I burst free from the mob. I saw Salem across the clearing, fighting to get to me, eyes locked on me across the snow. His eyes burned into me like a warning, even as the witches raked at his wings and his skin.

Witch bodies littered the ground around him. Someone grabbed my hair from behind. But just as she did, Salem let out a pulse of fiery magic that rippled over the snow. Dry heat swelled over the ice and trees, igniting them. I shielded my face from the blast. The snow melted beneath my feet.

When I looked up again, I could hardly breathe. The branches burned above me like torches. For one terrible moment, I thought this was it—the future I'd seen, of flames and death.

Heat seared my skin until I summoned my own magic to swell from my body—frigid water. Just as I unleashed a burst of freezing rain, Salem swooped down.

He wrapped his powerful arms around me, pulling me in close against his chest, and I wrapped my legs around his waist to hold on.

We flew low to the ground—barely a few feet off the snow, parallel to the earth—and I clung to him. Some of the low tree branches raked at his injured wings.

I clenched my jaw, trying to block out the pain that screamed in my body. "I thought you couldn't fly?"

"Not above the tree line. The wards would burn me there. But below the tree line is fine."

One of his wings slammed into a branch, and his muscles tensed.

I tried to peer over his shoulder. Between his beating wings, I saw a forest encased in ice and snow. The rain was starting to douse the trees, and smoke curled to the sky. The witches screamed—still alive.

Salem murmured into my ear, "For gods' sake, stop the freezing hail."

His chest felt colder than it should, and frost whitened

his eyebrows. I closed my eyes, using Salem's body to help subdue my magic.

"Where are we going?" I asked.

"We're getting the key." Without another word, he veered off the path.

But his flight seemed meandering. One of his wings looked completely ravaged.

I felt his heart beating faster, his jaw set like he was in pain.

"Do your wings hurt?" I cleared my throat. "Not that I care."

When he met my gaze, I saw a flash of something new in his eyes—an intense curiosity. Maybe even something like hope. It was quickly gone again with a mask of cold composure as he refocused on the path.

And there it was, the perplexing truth: it bothered me to see him hurt, this man who took my world from me. The man who would burn it all down to get what he wanted.

30

SALEM

S he tried to cover it up, but I saw it there in her face—the dawning, horrifying understanding that she cared about me.

I didn't think she realized she was my mate. Her loathing of me made that realization impossible.

But at this point, I had to live with the fact that I wouldn't be able to kill her. The horror of the image burned between my ribs, a roasting pit of shame.

"Why were there so many of them? You'd said there was one."

"This is a world where the very worst of things will multiply, and the very best wither and die. I made it that way, I think. I poisoned it."

"The witches reminded me of Beira. Except that she only has one eye."

That name—Beira—made my blood run cold. I couldn't speak of her. Even if I wanted to, her name would die on my tongue. She came from here, long ago, like I did. She despised me.

With Aenor's legs wrapped around me, body pressed

against mine, it was hard not to let my mind wander. In my most insane fantasy, I wanted her to be my queen. She'd sit by my side, resplendent in silks. She'd wield her power with abandon. At night, I'd send the rest of the court away. I'd pull off her gown and kiss her skin.

As if she could hear my thoughts, her pulse started racing.

But that feeling that we were perfectly in tune with each other—it was simply a distraction. A temptation to trap me here, when my destiny was in the heavens.

I'd focus on the pain instead. Sharp agony shot through my wings where the witches had smashed them. Each time a tree branch bashed me, my bones screamed. I wasn't sure the wings could keep me up in the air much longer at all. I thought one of the major bones was broken.

I scanned the forest floor beneath me, searching for the spot where I'd hidden the key—buried under the earth. As I swept through the trees, the snow thinned, and the air warmed around us.

I was so close now to finding Shahar. I could almost taste the glory of our heavenly throne. And now, I could almost see my sister's sad smile. She saved me once, and now I would save her. Not just from her watery prison, but from this entire terrible world.

At last, I spotted the gentle rise of the forest floor, and the trees thinned around me as a clearing opened up. There, I saw the circle of stones that had stood since the dawn of time.

It was here that I'd buried the key.

I tried to bring us down for a smooth landing. Instead, we landed hard on the earth and I rolled onto my broken wing. With one final crack of wing bone, it snapped. Pain exploded in my body.

I wouldn't be able to fly again until I'd healed it, nor could I make my wings disappear. I dusted the dirt off my bare chest. I looked ridiculous. If I ended up slaughtering King Tethra once and for all, perhaps I'd find a nice shirt in his wardrobe.

Aenor lay flat on her back, her blue hair spread out behind her. She narrowed her eyes, staring at my wing. "That looks bad."

It *definitely* bothered her. She wasn't even focusing on her own injuries, which were considerable.

She stood and dusted herself off, wincing. The witches had ripped through her clothes and into her flesh. Already, I could see the effects of the iron in her system, making her look nauseated. As soon as I found the key, I needed to get her to safety to heal her.

As I stared at her bloodied clothes, anger cracked through my body. "Perhaps before I leave here I will ignite it all. The witches' dying shrieks would delight me."

I hadn't actually realized that I'd said it out loud until she shot me a sharp look, her blue eyes piercing in the gloom of the forest. "You have disturbing hobbies."

I surveyed the clearing around me, finding that the hill and the rock formations were nearly as I remembered them. A circle of standing stones jutted into the dark forest air. The trees were almost entirely different. Gone were the ancient yews, replaced now by rowan and hawthorn trees.

One tree had been there since the dawn of time—an enchanted oak where I spent many a night when I wanted to get away from the castle. As soon as I found the key, I'd take care of Aenor in there. She gripped her side now, watching to see what I'd do next.

I stood in the center of the stones. Long ago, a yew had grown right where I stood, and it was near the yew that I'd buried the key. The tree had long since decayed, but if the key still existed, I'd be able to feel it in the earth. I knelt on the mossy ground, shoving my fingers into the soil. Then, to my immense relief, I felt the key's ancient magic snaking up my arm.

As my chest unclenched, I plucked it from the soil. It didn't look like a normal key, rather like a glowing white stone. I clutched it in my palm, letting the earthy magic whisper around me, a vortex of power. When I glanced up through the branches, I saw the magic shields shimmer away. Now, I could fly directly into the castle if I needed to.

I turned back to Aenor.

"We have what we need," I said. "But we need to heal each other before we can move on."

She was gazing over the tree branches at the castle, her arms folded. Was she considering how to get there without me?

She wouldn't tell me in a million years. I only knew that I had to watch out for her, keep her close to me. Which, as it turned out, was exactly my instinct anyway. She turned, peering in the other direction.

"They're coming." Her body tensed. "More witches."

I grabbed her by the elbow, which she immediately yanked out of my grasp.

"Just tell me where we're going," she said. "You don't have to guide me."

Gods, she was infuriating. "We're going to a tree."

"A tree." She sounded unimpressed.

And that was exactly why I hadn't said it out loud, given that it sounded idiotic.

"Just follow me." I crossed to the enchanted oak that stood just outside the ring of stones. The faintest glimmer of magic shimmered around it.

"Just to clarify," said Aenor, "there are killer witches coming for us, and we're going to a tree."

I didn't respond this time. Instead, I glanced up at the towering oak, its boughs stretching under the cloudy sky. It was at this point I realized I'd actually *missed* this place. After I'd been banished, I became so depraved that I could hardly form the thoughts to make sense of it. But I'd liked it here once. Perhaps I didn't want it to burn.

I pressed my hand against the bark. Magic sizzled along my arm, and the spirit of the tree whispered to me.

The true king has returned...

The words brought a faint smile to my lips.

In the bark, a hole began to open, widening to a hollow large enough to fit through. The edges of the opening pressed against my wings as I entered.

Stepping inside, I motioned to Aenor to join me. The enchanted tree opened up into a small, round cottage. Candles flickered in silver sconces, and tiny stars hung in the dark air above us, casting light over a single circular room. A bed curved into the wall, and a table was set with ancient fairy wine, bread, and fruit. A fire burned in a stony hearth, and wildflowers grew from the walls.

This had all been here since the dawn of history, but the wine would still taste sweet, the bread still fresh. This was my true home on earth. How had I forgotten it?

I turned to see Aenor stepping in behind me, her eyes wide. I felt absurdly pleased that I had managed to impress her with this. She belonged here, with me.

"What is this place?" she asked.

"My old home, the one away from the castle. The witches won't find us in here, so we can heal our injuries," I said. "This was once my little getaway from the palace."

"Where you brought your women when they weren't

allowed inside the palace? Those considered not sophisticated enough for the court, but good enough to bang?"

I frowned. "Yes, actually, but I wasn't going to go on
about my conquests because it seemed uncouth."

She sat on the bed, gripping her injured side. "Since
when did you care about being couth?"

I grabbed the wine off the small table and poured some
into a glass. I handed it to Aenor, then filled my little flask
with fairy wine.

Aenor took a sip, but her eyes were on the door as she
thought of her next step.

"Okay, let's get this over with," she said.

Close as I was to achieving my destiny, I didn't want to
leave here. I felt at ease in here in a way that I hadn't felt in
centuries. How different things would have been if I'd never
left.

"Stand up," I said.

She drained her glass in one long gulp, like she was
steeling herself for something terrible. Then she rose. "Are
you going to do that thing with your hand on my chest
again?"

"It's the best way to heal you."

It was, in fact, the best way for mates to heal each other.
Mates, in the fae world, were so few and far between that
most people didn't know much about them.

I put my hand on her chest, the heel of my palm
between her breasts. I let my magic pulse through my arm,
into her body. Standing this close to her was a dizzying
experience, like my senses were heightened. Her skin glistened gold, and her eyes shone like sunlight on the waves.

"It's working," she said quietly. "I can feel the iron
leaving my system."

Her cheeks were growing pinker now, her healthy color returning. Warmth spread in my chest. Even if she didn't want it all, I would return her magic to her. She might need it when I was gone. My gaze dipped to her lips, full and slightly parted as she looked at me. She *did* desire me, didn't she?

Maybe I would seduce her, just once. I could tell that she wanted me by the way her heart raced when we were closer, and her cheeks flushed a little. As I healed her, she held my gaze steadily.

I could lay her down beneath me and bring her such intense pleasure that she'd forget that she hated me. I'd kiss and lick her between her thighs until she couldn't remember her name.

It was the wrong thing to do, of course. I should leave her alone.

But since when did I take the high road?

My fevered thoughts were interrupted by the sound of the tree groaning around me. I pulled my hand away from Aenor and felt the air going cold.

"What's that sound?" asked Aenor. I crossed to the room's oak walls and pressed my hand against the wood—freezing now. Ice spread through the tree's veins. They were *killing* it.

"The witches have found us," said Aenor. "I can hear their music. They're surrounding us."

Alarm bells tolled in my mind. I didn't want them to destroy my home.

Anger simmered. "I'm going to kill them all now, once and for all. I'm going to sever their heads from their bodies and carve out their dreadful hearts." And then I would send them all to the Winter Witch, that repugnant canker. She'd spawned all these monsters in the first place.

I drew Lightbringer, and celestial flames flickered across its blade. "Wait in here."

"Uh, no," said Aenor. "You're still injured. I'm not."

"Fine." I couldn't think of a more perfect way to pass the time on earth than ripping apart the repulsive bodies of winter witches with my mate. Pity our fun together would be ending soon.

Pity, too, that my mate was biding her time before betraying me completely.

31

AENOR

I stood behind Salem as he pressed his palm against the oak. As the opening widened, I summoned my magic until strength imbued my limbs. Were these witches after me because of Salem, or did they try to kill anyone? I had no idea. All I knew was that they wanted me dead right now, and my sense of self-preservation filled me with a quiet violence.

As soon as I stepped out of the little tree cottage, the cold air hit me. The instant one of the witches lunged for me, I was slamming my fist into her head so hard that I thought I shattered her skull. Not many of them left now, just a small handful. I fought them with my bare hands, my feet, strength pounding through my blood.

Even with his broken wing, Salem was fighting with precision. And with one final arc of his blade, he severed the head of the last witch. Her body fell, writhing, to the forest floor.

I bit my lip, wondering if I could run fast enough to get to the castle before Salem. He was injured, after all, and I hadn't healed him yet.

But how would I even get in there? *Hello, guards, I'd like to conspire with someone you imprisoned for treason.*

Salem's eyes were on me, flickering from burned orange to a dusky blue. "Aenor," he murmured, his voice wrapping around me like a smoky caress, "I would love to know why it is that you keep looking at the castle."

My pulse sped up. If he learned the truth, my death would be more brutal than those he'd delivered to the witches. "Just looking out for more attackers. Like you said, the worst people thrived in this place, and there could be more monsters."

His powerful magic rolled off him like a warning.

I turned away from him, marching through the forest toward the castle. What I needed, before I healed him, was a way to get my message to the Merrow. *Send me the godsdamn sea glass.* If I could hear the Merrow's magic through the sea, I could communicate through water. I'd try a different, more direct message this time.

Hadn't Salem said that rivers and streams ran through the island?

I closed my eyes, trying to tune in to the feel of water, listening for its burbling sound. After a few moments, I felt a tug on my middle, pulling me east. I opened my eyes again, catching sight of a stream in the distance.

There we go.

I turned back to Salem, who was staring at me closely. "Do I need to force you to heal me?"

I ignored him for a moment. He'd said the water system ran into a moat, hadn't he? And the moat sometimes flooded the dungeon. That was my way to get a message to the Merrow.

"Let's not lose track of the Merrow. I want to run to the

stream over there to see if I can still hear his music before we move on. And I have to pee."

"Aren't you eager to help?"

"I want to end this as fast as I can, so I can move on and never see you again." *Lie.*

"Oh, but I was thinking of keeping you around." An amused smile curled his sensual lips. "Where else can I find such delicious, naked loathing?"

He prowled closer, his gait languid. "You know, I love nothing more than seducing a woman who hates me. There is no greater pleasure than the moans of a woman who has given in to temptation despite her better judgment." He winced. His mangled wings were apparently ruining his seduction ability.

Still, against my own better judgment, I felt heat tingling over my skin. "Like I said. You have weird hobbies."

He moved closer to me, his magic whispering over my body, and his eyes twinkled. "Perhaps, Aenor, I'll keep you with me, under my control for a while longer. I know you've imagined it already—me stripping your clothes off, teasing your beautiful body and making you come until you forget your own name."

My mind flashed back to that insane fantasy I'd had on the boat, the one where I was bending over before him, wild with desire. Heat rose in my body, making my chest flush, and I clenched my jaw. "I'll have you know I've thought of no such thing."

And all of a sudden I was talking like a Victorian duchess.

His lips quirked. "Your nostrils flare when you lie. Did you know that?"

With the intensity of his eyes, I felt completely exposed before him. He had a magnetic pull I couldn't ignore. In fact,

I had taken a step closer, compelled by the urge to press myself against him.

He reached for my waist, and I didn't pull away. Slowly, he stroked the back of his fingertips down my side. His touch left a trail of hot tingles in its wake, and my breath hitched.

He leaned down, his breath warming the curve of my throat. "I'd lick every inch of you until all that hatred dissolved from your mind, and the whole world would fall away. Everything except for the feel of my tongue on your body." His deep voice reverberated over my body, making my pulse race. "I'll make you shudder with pleasure, Aenor."

My breath was coming fast, and his heat warmed my body. His abs and chest muscles had gone taut, like he wanted satiation also.

Focus, Aenor. Focus. I gritted my teeth and forced myself to step away from him. I started to catch my breath. I knew my skin had flushed, and that Salem could tell what effect he was having on me.

"But you revolt me," I said.

He cocked his head. "Nostrils flaring, again."

As I took another step back from him, my blood started to cool a little. I forced those heated visions out of my mind. "Just tell me the layout so I can find the Merrow. We don't know he's in the castle." *Lie.* "How do the waterways connect?"

He crossed his arms, his gaze wary. "There's a moat around the base of the rocky hill, and a portcullis that leads directly into a watery tunnel, and then into the prison. Unless the Merrow is in the dungeon, he's unlikely to be connected to the water, I suppose. In any case, it will be guarded, and I have a better route in through the tower."

Okay. I just needed a little privacy.

"I have to pee," I declared again.

"And is that so important that you're unwilling to heal me and my broken wing?"

I swallowed. "My magic is all burned out. I can't heal you until I recharge."

It was the first lie that came to my mind. He cocked his eyebrow. He knew I was lying, but also didn't seem too concerned about it, his stance at ease. That unnerved me. He had a quiet confidence that no matter what happened, no matter what I did, he'd be in control.

And the strange thing was that he had every ability to force the truth out of me. He could invade my mind again. He could get me to fall to my knees and confess everything and kiss his feet while I was at it. He didn't.

"I'll just be a minute." I turned away from him, heading toward the stream.

As I walked, it occurred to me that he'd stopped invading my mind. Almost like he'd started to respect boundaries.

Gods, everything that had happened since I first met him was making this harder.

I didn't need to know about his beloved sister, or his damn cat, or that he'd comply with my boundaries when asked. I'd once vowed to rip him to pieces, and now the thought filled me with cold dread. In fact, an empty chasm was opening in my chest, sharp and cold.

Why had this task fallen to me, of all people?

A distant music beat through the forest as I approached the stream. It was relaxing, really. And slowly, the music started to burn away my sense of dread, growing louder.

It wasn't the music of a magical creature. No, the intense, wild music sizzled over my body and curled in my mind, making me feel a little delirious—like a cloud of warm euphoria was blossoming in my skull.

Truly, a kingdom of hedonism here.

Rowan boughs arched over the stream. Here, the air was warmer—humid, almost.

I stole a glance back at Salem and found that he had turned away from me, giving me privacy. I had to act fast. At any moment, he could come up behind me and discover what I was doing.

I dipped my fingertips into the water and started to swirl it around until it sparkled. Silver phosphorescence glimmered on the surface of the water. Just as I had before, I began to write a message.

God of the rivers, send my words to the Merrow through the water. I skimmed my fingertip over the river surface. I wrote, *Merrow,* in sparkly letters.

I bit my lip, trying to think clearly through the pleasurable beat of the music.

Another glance behind me told me that Salem was still facing the other direction.

Kneeling over the stream, I wrote, *I need the enchanted sea glass.*

I rested there, crouching. Would he have any idea what I was talking about?

I wrote, *The sea glass that can kill Salem. He's here. He's coming for you.*

I stared as the luminescent words simmered over the water's surface, then danced their way over the ripples. This seemed like my one chance to get a message to him, and I really wanted to get it right.

One more message before I returned to Salem. I dipped my fingertip in the water, inscribing the words in the stream.

I'm here. Looking for the weapon. We must stop Salem before the world burns. The final word blazed like an exploding star.

My heart raced. I was completely on my own here—an army of one.

With my breath coming fast and heavy, I waited to see if the Merrow could reply. By now, I was beyond stretching the credulity of how long it took to pee, but it was my only chance.

To my shock and delight, I caught an answer snaking and glittering along the surface of the water. I waited with bated breath until it reached me.

Kill him, or the world incinerates.

Frustration rose. Yes, I knew that. I needed the freaking weapon.

I waited to see if another explanation would arrive. The nearby music hummed along my skin, making me feel delirious.

After another minute, the explanation arrived in the form of a single word:

Anamfel.

Oh, for crying out loud. What the crap did that mean?

Come on, Merrow. Write something clear. Tell me how to get the weapon, how to kill him.

Frustrated, I rose and loosed a long sigh, still staring at the river. Waiting for another explanation. But no more words floated down the water. "Anamfel," I blurted. "Where do I find Anamfel? What is Anamfel?"

It was the tendrils of hot, smoky magic that told me Salem was near. When I turned around, my heart kicked up a beat. Salem leaned against a tree, his arms crossed. He was watching me.

"Who are you talking to?" His eyes twinkled with malice.

I cleared my throat. "Myself."

"And where did you hear the word Anamfel?"

My heart thundered. "It just... drifted on the wind. A distant voice."

"It's a mating festival. Do you have plans to meet someone there? You do keep me on my toes, Aenor. With whom would you like to mate?"

I stared at him, breath coming fast. I was waiting for him to invade my mind again, to force me to tell him whatever he wanted. "I don't even know what Anamfel means." For once, I was telling the truth.

"It's the mating festival in the forest. You can hear the music now." His deep voice reverberated over my skin.

Okay. So perhaps I'd get the sea glass there. It was the only clue I had, anyway.

That easy smile slipped from Salem's lips, and the air darkened around him. "Who are you meeting there?"

Somehow, he'd read this situation wrong. Did he think I was meeting a lover? Jealousy was blinding him. He wanted me to himself, didn't he?

What if I could use that? I could get him to let down his guard while I found the sea glass at the festival.

Desire could make him vulnerable. He wanted to have no attachments, and he didn't want to care for anything. He didn't want to love a cat, or his old house in the tree. He didn't want to love anything. Not when it was all going to burn.

And he definitely didn't want to care for me.

"I have no intention of meeting anyone there," I said. *Lie.* "I just wanted to know about the island." I bit my lip, swinging my hips a little as I moved closer to him.

His eyes burned as he watched me walk.

"But now that you've mentioned the festival, maybe we

should see it." I pressed up against him, my heart beating against his bare skin. "While my magic recharges."

Nearly imperceptible, a low growl reverberated from his throat.

"You're wasting my time, Aenor," he purred.

But I'd distracted him, hadn't I? His warm magic pulsed around me, protective and sensual.

"What's the rush?" I looked up at him, burying dread with the most seductive smile I could muster—the smile of a morgen luring her prey to his death. "You said you'd make me moan, didn't you?"

With my eyes locked on his, I grabbed his hand and started to lead him toward the music. "I think the music is calling to me."

The truth mixed with lies, until I found it hard to remember what was real anymore. The only thing clear to me was that I felt like my heart was splintering.

32

AENOR

W e were coming up to the edge of a clearing, and half-naked dancers flitted between the trees. The music *was* luring me with a primal desire to dance.

In the center of a clearing, a fire roared, dark tendrils of smoke curling into the air. The music pulsed through my blood, beckoning me closer. As we approached, the sky seemed to change, darkening to ashy rose and indigo. Twilight was falling over us...

It wasn't the right time for dusk, was it? As I looked up at the sky, I had the sense that Salem and Mag Mell were linked. The dying evening light and the gold of the fire blazed over the bodies of the dancers. I felt like a moth moving toward the fire, drawn by its brightness.

I scanned the crowds, trying to stay alert. Revelers were having sex against the trees, dancing naked around the fire. Where was I supposed to find the weapon?

When I turned back to Salem, I found his eyes burning with coral and blue hues that matched the skies. He looked at peace here. I thought if he only had his cat and his little tree house, he *might* have some semblance of happiness.

And there it was again, that empty cavern opening in my chest. When I took in his broken wing, I felt an over-whelming urge to heal him. The instinct to press my hand against his chest and fill him with my magic was almost overpowering.

Why heal someone I was about to kill? Dizziness slammed into me, a feeling of wrongness. It was like an iron thread was tugging me by my middle, forcing me closer to him. His seductive magic skimmed my body, and I wanted to wrap my arms around him.

But if I was going to find this weapon, I needed to get away from him.

My silent prayers were answered when a woman with gleaming platinum hair ran for us, interrupting my thoughts. Apart from a sheer thong, she was practically naked. Gossamer wings swept down her back. She smiled at Salem, then slid her arms around his neck.

I felt a bizarre pang of jealousy. "I see what you mean by hedonism."

Salem pulled the woman's hands off him. "You fail to spark my interest."

Undeterred, she moved closer. Her body *glowed.* "King. Mate with me. It's Anamfel. *Fill me.*"

More of these nymphs were now running from the festi-val, drawn by his smell or his magic. They were laughing, eyes bright.

"King!" one of them shouted. "The fallen king!"

"How do they all know you're the king?" I asked. "Are they all a billion years old as well?"

He shot me a sharp look. "They smell it on me, and they feel it in my magic. My soul is bound to this land." His gaze slid down my body, and I knew he was imagining me naked. "But *you* are the one who lured me here, and I have no interest in the rest."

Before I could reply, the silver-haired woman danced over to me, then grabbed me by the hands.

She pulled me toward the fire, and I didn't object. At last, I had a moment away from Salem. Quickly, I got lost in the throng of half-naked dancers. The music swelled in the air, a deep and sensual song that nearly made me forget why I was here. I nearly tripped over a couple rutting on the ground, the woman on all fours.

Life surrounded me, but death was my mission.

I scanned the revelers, trying to stay alert while my mind was growing increasingly delirious. With the music and the golden light, the air swelled with an erotic heat. Around me, fae were kissing, writhing, and stroking each other.

We wove between bodies that glowed golden in the flickering firelight.

Remember your mission, Aenor.

Over the flames, I glanced at Salem. His hungry eyes were on me. Even with the nymph-like women draping themselves on him, their bodies demanding, he was looking only at me.

The heat of the flames warmed my skin, and I searched frantically for a messenger or a sign of the sea glass.

But as soon as I started pulling away from the silver-haired woman, she grabbed my wrist. All the delirious wildness was gone from her eyes, replaced by a keen awareness.

She pulled me in closer in a hug, and then whispered in my ear, "The Merrow sent me from his prison. Lure Salem away from the crowd, and then plunge this into his heart." She slid a piece of glass into my palm.

Excitement and fear crackled over me, and I slid the

glass into the pocket of my skirt. "How am I supposed to overcome someone as powerful as he is? He can control my mind."

"It's Anamfel. Everyone wants to mate. You're overcome by the music, or at least you can fake it. Seduce him until he lets down his guard. Do this, or the world turns to ash. You have no choice."

My mind was ablaze. I glanced at the fire, a reminder of what lay ahead of us if Salem succeeded.

The silver-haired nymph snatched a silver goblet out of the hand of a dancer. Then she handed it to me, moving in close again to whisper, "Get rid of your inhibitions. This will help. Do it, now."

My hands were shaking as I took a sip of the wine, steeling myself for the assassination that would come next.

As soon as the wine hit my tongue, I realized it wasn't ordinary wine. When I swallowed it, a wave of ecstasy rippled through my body. My panicked thoughts grew quieter, and I felt connected to the earth beneath my feet. The music pulsed in my mind, dulling my worries. I touched the shard of sea glass in my pocket. I knew what I had to do.

"Good," she said, smiling now.

I drained the glass, then the nymph snatched it from my hand. "That's enough."

Not a care in the world...

I danced away from her, my bare feet padding on the soft earth.

With the wine in my system, I felt the urge to pull off my clothes, to let the forest air kiss my bare skin. We were wild creatures here. Heat warmed my cheeks. That nymph had been my savior, and now I'd save the world.

When I reached Salem, the women surrounding him fell

away from him, like a sea parting. It was all coming together. This was my destiny, and I'd been born for this.

When I reached him, I grabbed his hands. I smiled at Salem, lowering my chin with my seductive morgen look. Desire sent my pulse racing.

It was hard to truly seduce someone without actually being turned on.

I traced my hand down my body, then toyed with the hem of my skirt, lifting it a little. "I like Anamfel."

His eyes were on my thighs. His magic, stroking my body, had a dark, erotic feel.

With the way he was looking at me, like he wanted to rip my clothes off and fill me, I could feel the hot blush spreading on my cheeks, my heartbeat racing. "Like you said, I hate just about everything about you. But maybe you're right. There's something in the air with this festival."

"I don't recall saying that." His voice had grown husky, eyes burning. "But you have my attention."

I licked my lips, and his eyes locked on my mouth. "And maybe we hate each other, but you *are* right here."

"*Right here?* Is that my most appealing attribute?" he purred. "Not the fact that I have the body of a god, or a perfect face? I find that hard to believe."

I let out a shuddering breath. "We have a few minutes, don't we?"

"A few minutes? I'm afraid you still underestimate me."

I was so close to him now that my breasts brushed against his muscled chest, and his muscles went completely taut. When I looked up into his eyes, I felt like he was peering into my very soul. He could take me apart with erotic torment, then slowly piece me together again.

The wine and the heat from his powerful body lit me up, and my thighs clenched. But he was broken, and I wanted him whole. Without thinking about the consequences, I pressed my hand against his chest to heal him. When my palm made contact with him, a wave of hot pleasure rushed through my body. Every inch of my skin felt sensitive, my breasts peaking.

The hungry look he was giving me was stoking a need I wanted to ignore.

His wings stretched out behind him, glowing as I healed him. My magic twined with his, and the majestic beauty of his wings made my breath catch. He closed his eyes, letting out a low sigh.

As I healed him, I breathed in his scent. My heart beat faster, and I realized his smell was like an aphrodisiac to me.

I watched my magic snaking over his body, caressing his wings. Something about it seemed... *perfect.* Meant to be.

Lure him into the woods. End it all.

When I'd finished healing him, I pulled my hand from his chest, and his wings shimmered away.

He reached for my waist, running the back of his knuckles up and down my side. Tingles raced over my skin. He leaned down and whispered, "Let's come away from all these people."

His breath warmed the shell of my ear. Already, my body was aching with need for him.

He leaned down and scooped me up, carrying me away from the festival. I wrapped my arms around his neck, and gods, I wanted to wrap my legs around him. Close to his body, I felt his heart pounding.

When I glanced down at his chest, where I had to stab him, my thoughts sharpened into a crystalline arrow point.

Kill the beautiful man.

Away from the other revelers, he stopped walking, and I slid down his body. "I have you alone, at last," he murmured.

"Take off your clothes. I've been desperate to see you naked since I first had you under my control."

That command made heat pulse between my thighs. Gods, I wanted him to see me naked. I wanted to get down in the dirt and let him claim me...

But I was here for another reason, and I had to remember that.

Something electric crackled between us as I unbuttoned the top of my shirt. His eyes dipped to the swell of my breasts, and I took another step away from him.

His gaze drank in my body. He was hungry for me.

As his magic stroked my skin, licking my body and warming me like firelight, warmth pulsed between my thighs.

I backed up against a hawthorn tree and unbuttoned another button. The forest air kissed my skin. Salem prowled closer, then pressed his hands on the tree trunk on either side of my head.

"Take it off, Aenor." His deep, erotic tone skimmed my exposed skin.

One more button, and his eyes dipped to my breasts, nipples hardening under his gaze. They were aching for his touch.

He was boxing me in, looking down at me with wonder, and fire blazed in his eyes. "Just one temptation," he murmured softly, "before my destiny awaits."

He lowered his head and grazed his mouth against my throat, and I nearly moaned. Pleasure rippled out from where he kissed me. I tried to remember my mission...

I touched his well-built chest, and his muscles tensed. They were like steel under his smooth skin.

Slowly, he brushed his lips over my neck. I arched my throat, making myself vulnerable to him. I felt strangely protected around him. Safe, for reasons that must have been insane. As his tongue moved over my skin, sexual need burned through my body.

Or the world will burn...

I reached into my pocket and grabbed the sea glass. Ice spread through me.

In one swift movement, I lifted it to his heart.

Now, it was all over.

33

SALEM

M y mind nearly went blank as I stared down at the gleaming shard of blue glass pressing into my chest. One of her hands was curled around the back of my neck.

With the other, she'd jabbed the sharp tip of the sea glass into my skin, just below my sternum. One sharp thrust upward, and it would be in my heart. Every muscle in my body was rigid, my desire to live warring with the instinct not to hurt her.

So *this* was Aenor's plan. She hadn't wanted to seduce me, but to kill me. Why in the name of the gods had I trusted a morgen's seduction? This was what they did. What an idiot I was.

I tried to summon my magic to invade her mind, to stop her—but that little point of glass in my chest was already draining my power.

Of course she'd wanted to kill me. I'd taken her world from her—her magic, her kingdom, her mother... She'd sworn vengeance. I'd forced her to work for me, mocking her as I did. I'd even invaded her mind, making her lust for me. I'd imagined making her strip for my pleasure. Of course this was all part of her plan.

Since when had I ever let my guard down like that so easily?

And yet... she hadn't killed me yet. Was that the mate bond stopping her?

A single streak of black blood streamed down my chest. Already, I could feel the weapon poisoning me, pain radiating through my chest like a toxin.

"Well, Aenor. I thought we were just starting to get comfortable with each other."

Her jaw was set firmly, eyes focused. Her entire body had gone rigid. With her shirt halfway unbuttoned, I could see her chest rising and falling fast. "Why can't I do it?" she asked.

She still didn't know.

"I feel as if you are asking me to advise you on how to better kill me. I'm not inclined to do so."

Her eyes gleamed with tears. "I was talking to myself."

"Only one person can kill me."

"It's me." Her eyes shone. "So why can't I do it? I *have* to. I've seen what happens if I don't. I've killed plenty of evil men before. You're the worst. I don't understand why I can't kill you."

"I still feel as if you want me to convince you to jam that into my heart. I won't help you with that, I'm afraid."

Sweat beaded on her forehead, and she gritted her teeth. "It's like... I feel safe around you even though it makes no sense. It's objectively insane, given our history. Is this your magic? The fruit you gave me?" She bit her lip. "Or is it the festival and the wine... Maybe both. I just feel like... we should be..." She seemed like she was coming unglued, trying to convince herself of something that fate wouldn't let her do. "Like we should be together? This doesn't make sense. I just need to fight through the confusion and do it. Okay. I can do this."

"I've never been less enthusiastic about giving someone a pep talk." She wouldn't do it, would she? She was my *mate*.

She closed her eyes and shook her head, and a tendril of blue hair fell in her face, catching in her long eyelashes. I brushed it out of her eyes, and she opened them again. With the way she was looking up at me, so lost, I wanted to pull her closer to me.

There was just this weapon between us, getting in the way. "Drop it, Aenor. You won't be able to do it." Pain radiated out from the spot where she was piercing me.

"Why can't I?"

"Perhaps your mind is clouded by my devastatingly divine appearance. Don't feel bad, Aenor. My beauty has shattered the wills of more formidable women."

She narrowed her eyes at me, looking like she was about to change her mind and ram the glass all the way into my heart once and for all. Perhaps this was not the time to irritate her.

What she didn't know was that the mating bond meant every instinct in her body would tell her not to do it. She was the only one who could kill me, but her own mind would stop her from doing it.

She grunted with frustration, staring into my eyes with intense hatred. "Do you know how many hearts I've cut out?"

"Lots, I'm sure. But not this one, Aenor. This one you want to keep safe. You don't want to hurt me."

"Don't use your mind control on me."

"I'm not."

Her hands shook as she lowered the sea glass. "Gods have mercy. This is all screwed up. But I'm not done with this. We'll come back to this." She shoved the sea glass into her pocket. "I can still kill you."

Gods, I wanted to pull her into my little tree cottage and make her gasp.

Her dark eyebrows knitted. "I'm going to stick on you like shine on gold. I'm going to convince you not to unleash hell on earth. And if you get close to the driftwood cage before we figure out a solution, I'll kill you. I will cut your damn heart out. Just not yet. I need to know you'll really do it before I act."

I grabbed her hand and pressed it against my heart. Her magic pulsed into me, healing me. I let out a shuddering sigh at the feel of this intimacy. Her flowery scent washed over me. I wanted to nestle my face between her legs.

"Hmmm," I said softly. "Perhaps I can be convinced not to." This was a lie. I just wanted her close to me. I wanted her to look at me the way she had when I'd brushed the hair from her eyes.

I'd give in to this one last, perfect temptation before I moved on from this world.

Her lips were only a few inches from mine, her eyes heavily lidded, and she whispered, "I loathe you very much."

"But instinct tells you I'll keep you safe. You know that, don't you?" I'd never seen anyone so beautiful in my life. I had a wild, insane impulse to give her what she wanted, to promise her that I'd leave my own sister in eternal torment at the bottom of the sea. She was mine, and I could hardly think of leaving her.

Instead, I leaned down and kissed her deeply, and the emptiness in my chest started to melt away.

She was mine, and she was the last thing I'd have on earth.

34

AENOR

I parted my lips, welcoming the kiss, and that ache started building again, a rhythmic pulsing in my core. There was still time to persuade him...

Bizarrely, he was right. I did feel safe around him, like he'd burn the world down to keep me from being hurt.

Or was it just that—well—he'd burn the world down.

His tongue swept in as the kiss deepened, and his dark, sexual magic curled around me. Every inch of my skin felt alive, burning all resistance from my mind. The forest air kissed my skin, full and warm.

His hand was on my waist, keeping me exactly where he wanted me, and my body hummed with desire. My breasts felt full against the damp cotton of my shirt, my entire body acutely sensitive with craving for him.

God of temptation...

He pulled away from the exquisite kiss, his eyes smoldering as he gazed into mine. His muscles looked rigid with anticipation.

My shirt, already partially unbuttoned, was hanging off my shoulders now.

"You need to finish taking that off," he said.

At this point, I didn't care that we were out in a forest with other people nearby. I didn't care about anything except satiating my need.

I unbuttoned the rest of my shirt, and the warm forest air kissed my exposed skin. Salem's eyes burned as he watched me. Then he slid his hand up from my waist to palm one of my breasts. He caressed and stroked it until my nipple went rock-hard against his palm.

He leaned down again, his mouth on my throat. Heat radiated out where he kissed me. One hot, lazy kiss after another seared the skin. I tilted my head back as I gave myself to him. His enjoyment of my body was apparent. Now, I wanted the skirt off.

With excruciating slowness, he slid his hand down my bare skin to the waistband of my skirt. I arched my back as he dipped his fingers inside the waist. He trailed his fingertips from one hip to another, teasing me as he kissed my throat. His touch was unhurried, drawing out my desire. My hips started rocking as a deep ache built between my thighs.

"Salem," I whispered.

He let out a low laugh. "I am going to enjoy taking my time with you, Aenor."

Slowly, he unbuttoned my skirt, and it slid off to my ankles. He swept his gaze down, taking in my blue silk panties. His muscles had tensed completely, and he looked for a moment like he was about to lose control.

But he still kept stroking me—slow and lazy over the front of my panties. The touch swept a little lower, moving over my hipbone. Liquid heat rushed through my core. Oh gods, I wanted him to fill me. He slid one of his fingers into the top of my panties, circling lightly over the hollow of my hip.

"Salem." My voice cracked; I was desperate for satiation.

Another low laugh as he delighted in my desperation. I wanted to force his hand lower, between the apex of my thighs.

But those slow, lazy strokes over my hipbone just made my blood pound harder. I wrapped my arms around his neck, and he kissed me again—a slow, sensual kiss.

His touch on my hip was infuriatingly light, the other a possessive hand on my waist, rooting me in place where he wanted me.

He pulled away from the kiss. "Tell me what you want," he whispered.

"You."

He pulled his thumb from my hip, then stroked his knuckles over the front of my panties. Gods, just a little lower...

Molten heat surged. My nipples were painfully sensitive as they brushed against his bare chest.

Salem was born to torment, and that's what he was doing to me. In the clearest hollows of my mind, a single thought—*Keep the sea glass close. Protect it.*

But another, lower stroke of Salem's fingertips burned those thoughts away, teasing me with light movements between my thighs. I widened my legs and moved against his hand, demanding more.

"Salem..." I whispered. This was an exquisite sort of torture, my entire body humming with raw sexual need.

"Is there something you need from me?" Amusement tinged his voice.

Maybe I didn't need to move at his pace.

My chest heaving, I leaned back against the tree so he could watch me. I slid my hands into my panties, then pulled them down to my ankles. Once again he traced his gaze down my body, taking me in completely, and his body emitted a glow of fiery light. He was burning up with need as much as I was.

His muscles had gone completely tense, and he let out a low, appreciative growl when his gaze reached the apex of my thighs. When his eyes met mine, I saw in them a burning possessiveness, an unmistakably masculine craving for me.

His wings spread out behind him, and the gold that shot through the dark feathers seemed to glow. Wonder bloomed in my chest. Right now, he didn't seem like a being meant for this world...

I reached out, touching the tips of his feathers, and he closed his eyes, his breath hitching. When he opened them again, wild desire burned. "You know what I like, instinctively. And I think I know what your body craves."

In one smooth motion, he turned me around to face the tree. He pressed his hard body against me, every glorious male inch of him.

"I need to explore you more." He moved his hand up to cup my breast, moving his thumb over it. Tingles radiated out from his touch. I leaned back into him. My body swelled for him.

And yet—I had that feeling again of bliss... of perfection together. It was the same as when I'd slept in the boat, curled up in his arms.

He traced his other hand slowly down my body, sliding it down my belly, over my hips, until he reached the apex of my thighs. He groaned low into my neck as he felt my slick arousal.

He touched me in light circles, feeling my heat, teasing me until I couldn't think clearly anymore, until my mind burned.

He kissed my neck, and pleasure crashed through me.

With one hand, he spread me open, and I was about to scream with need. He slid a finger inside me, and I moaned. I writhed against his hand, in and out, clenching around him. I flung my arms backward, curling them around his neck. The desperate noises I was making now sounded animal.

"Salem," I managed. "Please…"

A low, dark chuckle from him skimmed over my skin. I could hardly remember how words worked now. I only knew I needed that feeling of fullness.

He pulled his hand away and turned me around again— the movement faster now. He was desperate for me. I hadn't even realized he'd taken off his pants until now, but I took in the sight of him, his stunning, masculine perfection. He reached under my bum, and I wrapped my legs around him as he lifted me against the tree.

"Aenor." There was a wild hunger in his voice now. His eyes were on mine as he slid into me slowly, filling me completely.

Oh gods yes.

His magic snaked over my body in ripples of pleasure, as he moved in me—slowly, deeply.

Gods help me, I felt safe with him. I felt like I belonged with him, like we were *made* for each other. We moved with each other, pleasure spiraling into my body as he pounded into me. With each deep thrust, I felt myself arcing higher to a perfect completion, a deep soul connection. He kissed me, and this time it was urgent, demanding. He was losing control as I was.

I dragged my nails down his back, moaning his name as I shuddered against him, pleasure shattering my mind into a thousand tiny pieces of sea glass.

35

AENOR

With my arms wrapped around him, I caught my breath. My body glistened with a light sheen of sweat.

"What are the scars?" he whispered in my ear.

I'd almost forgotten about them—the scars carved in my skin long ago, after I'd lost my power.

But I didn't really want to go into it now. "Left by some bad demons."

His muscles tensed for a moment. "I hope you cut their hearts out."

I smiled. "Oh, I did."

Slowly, Salem released me to the ground. The ripples of pleasure still pulsed through my body, and I caught my breath. His eyes were still on me, half-lidded, arms warm around my body. He was looking down at me with a look of complete satisfaction.

Salem's heart beat against me, loud and echoey like a sacrificial drum. His body felt like it was burning against me, and his smoky magic curled around me.

But when I caught a flash of silver hair moving through

the trees, my blood turned to ice. There she was, the Merrow's agent—a reminder of my task: kill him, or the world burns.

Gods, had she been watching us?

With the cold chill of reality seeping into my consciousness, icy dread spread out over my mind like webs of frost.

"What's wrong?" Salem asked into my hair.

His powerful arms were wrapped around me, pulling me in close to his chest like he never wanted to release me.

And yet reality was eating away at the warm bond between us.

I still had so many unanswered questions.

"When I made a teeny-tiny sacrifice to the god of the sea," I began, "and I spilled a little bit of blood into the ocean—why did that bother you so much?"

"Gods are petty creatures, demanding love," he said. "Demanding that you prove yourself. Petty and jealous, more beast than angel."

My mind flicked back to what he had told me, about the burning human sacrifices in the cave. "But people sacrificed to you when they thought you were a god."

"You really know how to kill a mood, do you know that?" he murmured into my ear. Then, more coldly, "I can't answer that. It is what it is, and I've told you what I am. I've told you I poison everything. You know that I'm destruction embodied. I don't belong in this world, and neither does Shahar." He stepped away from me and pulled on his pants.

Shahar... He was already moving on to saving his sister. Desperation spiraled through me. "The prophecy, the visions—my own magic is telling me that complete destruction awaits if you save your sister. I need you to find another way. We need more time."

"Time? You want me to leave her, tormented in darkness, drained of her magic, because of visions and prophecies?"

"I don't know how to say this without sounding insensitive, but she's been there for a hundred years—what's another week?" That was phrased badly, perhaps.

I snatched my underwear off the forest floor and stepped into them.

The air seemed to go cold around us. "I have a destiny, Aenor, and if I don't fulfill it within a few days, it's all over. And it begins with saving Shahar."

So this wasn't just about love for his sister. "A destiny," I repeated.

"Which you have done your best to thwart. Your seduction didn't help."

"My seduction?" I was on the verge of saying *you started it*, but that sounded outrageously childish.

"Do you plan to keep repeating everything I say?" he asked.

Oh, screw you, Salem.

I kept one eye on my skirt, then snatched it up off the ground. What had I been thinking? He was right. He never lied about what he was. He was destruction embodied— chaos and death personified in one beautiful, masculine form.

Had he ever pretended otherwise?

Salem's eyes narrowed as he watched me slip my hand into my pocket, reaching for the sea glass to make sure it was there. He understood I was keeping the weapon near me. Nothing had changed. I still had to kill him if he wouldn't listen to me.

I took a deep breath, searching around for my shirt. My mission here had gone off task *just a tad*. My thoughts in this enchanted forest had become completely confused until I actually believed that I was safe with him, that I belonged with him.

In reality, the exact opposite was the truth.

"I don't know what I was thinking." I gestured at the tree where we'd just been entwined only moments before. "What just happened? It was the wine. And the festival. Nothing more. I feel nothing for you."

"Of course, Aenor. It was the wine." His voice was frigid as his wings spread out behind him. He looked down at me, eyes cold as ice. "We are still mortal enemies. I wouldn't dream of anything else."

I glared at him, pulling on my shirt. Frost spread through my chest. "I will stop you before you get to the driftwood cage."

His lips curled in a lethal smile. "Then you'll need all the help you can get." He plucked the ring off his finger and grabbed my hand to slide it onto mine.

I thought I saw a flicker of hurt in his eyes as they shifted from coral to blue. This was a dark sort of wedding, a ceremony threaded with betrayal.

"The thing is, Aenor, I'm not sure I need you anymore. You've healed me, and given the number of times you looked at the castle, I can only assume he's there—in the dungeons, where the water reaches."

I felt like my chest had been hollowed out with a jagged rock as I reached into my pocket.

Do it, Aenor.

But it was like my hand would not move to complete its task. Ice chilled my blood as his wings spread out behind him, resplendent in the fiery twilight. I finally managed to snatch the sea glass from my pocket, but his wings were already beating the air, his eyes on the sky above him.

My breath stopped as I watched him take to the skies, flying through the canopy of leaves.

My heart was shattering into tiny pieces.

The extra magic from the ring surged through my veins, an overwhelming rush of power that made me want to tear through the forest. It made me want to drown everything. Now, the twilight seemed too bright, garish. The sound of the birds in the trees was deafening, the rustling leaves like someone screaming in my ear.

I tried to control the rush of magic, focusing on my connection to the earth. I leaned back against the tree trunk, modulating my magic through the ground. The power, my old power, fully returned to me, was hard to control.

When I opened my eyes again, I caught a glimpse of Salem's wings, slipping away above the trees.

When I looked down, I saw the silver-haired nymph staring at me, furious.

"You had one simple task," she said. "Kill him, not fuck him. I mean, you could have done both, but the important part was killing him."

My magic vibrated through my body. "I just couldn't do it. It was like it was some kind of magic."

Fury burned in her eyes. "Of course killing your mate isn't supposed to be easy, but you had to do it. You know the consequences if you don't."

Your mate.

It was like she had slammed her fist into my stomach and flattened all the air out of me.

My mate? The Nameless One I'd always hated, the man who'd killed Mama...

The world seem to tilt beneath my feet, until I wasn't quite sure where I was anymore. And yet it made *sense.*

All the pieces were sliding into place in my mind—that

feeling of safety when I was with him. My wild desire for him. The reason he'd never killed me, why I couldn't kill him.

That weird way we could heal each other. He *knew,* didn't he? But he'd still left me here. Because like he'd said —he'd never pretended to be anything other than evil. Having a mate didn't change that.

My entire body felt cold and numb, my mind a dark hollow. The word "mate" echoed off the confines of my skull, like a drumbeat off cave walls.

"Oh? You didn't know? Well, yeah. Now you're up to speed." Her gaze flicked up to the palace that towered over the forest. "Look, you're the one with the soul bond to him. What's he doing now?"

When somebody asked you a question like that, about your soul bond to another person, you wanted to be able to say something empathic, give a glimpse of their softer side or vulnerability.

But that was not the case with my soulmate, the actual devil. "He's going to find the Merrow in the dungeon. He will greet him with an excruciating, mind-bending torture until the sorcerer confesses the location of the driftwood cage. We can only hope to get to the Merrow before he finishes." I gritted my teeth. "It's possible he can also take the Merrow with him, and torture him on the way."

"Gods below."

I nodded at the river. "I can get us there faster through the water. Try to keep up."

My magic electrified my body, and I turned, running for the river. My bare feet pounded against the earth, the sound booming. I was exploding with power.

I could hear the other woman behind me, just barely keeping up, her breath heavy.

The sea glass hung heavy in my pocket, brushing against my thigh. The wind whipped over my body as I ran. I could see the water now, glistening nearby. With a spell and my overpowering magic, I could get us to the castle fast.

When I reached the river's edge, I dove in. A few moments later, the nymph followed.

I pulled the sea glass from my pocket and sliced my thigh.

Blood pooled in the water around me. "God of the rivers and sea, take us to Salem."

The river rushed and swirled around us, an orchestra of light on the water. Then, at the speed of a furious typhoon wind, the waters carried us. In the wild surge of water, I gripped the sea glass. I would be ready this time. That feeling, that surety of safety, was nothing but an illusion. It was a trick of the mating bond, nothing more. A dumb, animal instinct.

Get to Salem. Stop him, by whatever means.

The river seethed and frothed around me, and I gave in to its power as it carried us.

But was I too late? I'd never met anyone so determined. My darling mate would burn the world down to get what he wanted. His destiny, whatever it was, mattered to him more than anything.

At last, the rushing river carried us into the moat that ringed the castle. I grabbed for a rock to stop myself. Dripping wet, I hoisted myself up to the banks of the moat.

Anger at Salem was giving me clarity now.

He'd *left* me. Why did that feel so terrible?

As I pulled myself onto the bank, the nymph followed, gasping for breath. Then she fell onto her hands and knees, coughing up water.

A drawbridge spanned the moat, but a heavy metal

portcullis blocked the main entryway. And beside it stood an armed guard. Salem had the distinct advantage of flying in from above, probably unnoticed.

Sucking in a deep breath, I looked up at the castle. Its dark, spindly spires speared the heavens, but vines had overgrown them. The statues and gargoyles jutting from the castle were worn with time, many of them broken. A ruin of a place.

And Salem wasn't anywhere in sight.

"How do we get in?" I asked.

The nymph caught her breath and stood. "I'll get us in. Follow me."

Her bare feet slapped against the wooden drawbridge as she hurried over it. Just before the gate, she stopped and grinned at the guard. "Hi, Mallour. Are we still meeting for dinner later?"

He grinned at her, blushing. "Yes. Oysters and cheese."

"Mmm, oysters." She giggled. "I forgot my shoes inside; could you let me in?"

"Of course, Lyria."

Within moments, the portcullis began to slide up. We darted inside, and I let her lead the way. Within moments, we were in an all-out sprint—but luckily, the castle seemed deserted.

My legs carried me fast, my sea magic rippling through my body with wild abandon.

I followed Lyria through a vaulted castle hallway, its stony walls cracked. Flowering vines seemed to be over-taking the place. Spheres of pearly light hung in the air like dim stars, lighting the way.

One turn after the next in the byzantine halls had me feeling that we were lost, until Lyria stopped abruptly. She stood before a small wooden door inset in a wall.

When she pressed her hands against it, magic burned out from her fingertips, flashing blue over the surface of the door. And then—nothing happened.

She cursed under her breath. "They've changed the magical signature."

Who needed a magical signature when you had the force of seven oceans in your body? I was bursting to use my magic. "Stand back."

As soon as she moved out of the way, I lunged forward, magic igniting my muscles. I slammed my foot into the door, splintering it into tiny pieces.

Lyria stared at me for a moment. "Okay, well. Do that again to the skulls of anyone who tries to stop us." She rushed through the doorway, leading me into a narrow, musty stairwell going down.

She motioned for me to follow her down the stairs.

My breath dragged in my lungs as I whispered, "How did the Merrow end up imprisoned here?"

"He tried to stop King Tethra. You know, when he sent his assassins after Salem and you."

My mind whirled. How were Tethra and Salem connected?

Again I was struck by the feeling that I'd only scratched the surface in understanding my *darling* mate.

36

AENOR

A s we got to the bottom of the stairs, darkness enveloped us. My legs plunged into cold water, about a foot deep. It was at this point I realized with a growing sense of horror that I could no longer hear the Merrow's music.

The nymph snapped her fingers, and twinkling lights appeared above us. The light glimmered over dark water that streamed through a long corridor, pouring into the cells. The smell down here was overpowering, like rotten flesh and death. I wanted to vomit.

Apart from the sound of flowing water, we found the dungeon eerily silent. As we crossed deeper inside, I scanned and searched for the Merrow in a cell. As I did, I glimpsed the pitiful fae creatures who languished in their cells, crammed together, many of them ancient-looking, emaciated. The music of their magic was hardly audible.

From the far side of the corridor, the moat ran into the dungeon, flowing through a hole in the wall. Water filled the bottoms of the cells at least a foot deep.

Gods, it was awful here. Some of the fae were tied with

their hands behind their backs. Others were tied to wooden posts that jutted from the stone ground, bodies limp, looking half-dead, skeletal.

But worst of all, I found not a single sign of Salem, nor could I hear his magic. Lyria swore as she led me to the end of the corridor. There, one cell door stood open in the water.

And as we peered inside, we found no one.

Lyria thrust her fingers into her silver hair, looking like she was about to pull it out. "He's taken him. And if the king catches us here, will both die."

"What are King Tethra's plans? I don't understand. What do Salem and this king have to do with each other? Are they working together? I need some answers."

She chewed a fingernail. "Tethra and Salem? They can't stand each other. King Tethra usurped Salem's throne eons ago. Took this whole kingdom from him after he was banished. But he let the kingdom languish, and it's in ruins now. King Tethra thought he could grow stronger and build the kingdom's strength by making himself stronger. He was taking quicksilver supplements prescribed by fae doctors."

I blinked. "Mercury? He was drinking mercury? It causes brain damage."

"Yeah, so the king basically has holes in his brain now. He's obsessed with raising the Fomorian army to take over the world. And one of his advisors told him how to do it. He said to send a message to Salem. You know the whole legend."

"Nope. I have no idea what you're talking about."

"The Fomorians once lived in this kingdom. The first king of Mag Mell defeated them, and drove them all down to the center of the earth. Once, they were normal fae, like us. But under the earth's surface, they grew twisted. Fiery.

And now they want revenge. King Tethra thinks he can raise them and control them. But no one can control them."

"Okay. And get to the part where Salem is involved."

"The legend was that only a god's magic could keep the earth sealed, keep the Fomorians trapped in its core. Every now and then, one of the Fomorians would slip out, start burning things. Lighting cities on fire. The Great Fire of London? That was a Fomorian. So the Merrow found a way to seal it up again, at least for a while. You helped him, remember? Shahar's magic was enough to seal them inside. Without it, everyone would have turned to dust."

And that was what awaited us now. "Go on."

"But her magic is weakening, and it's not working as well now. And then the rumors started spreading. Destroy the driftwood cage, and the Fomorians will rise. Tethra is trying to make it happen."

"So Tethra was using Salem?"

She nodded. "He knew Salem would stop at nothing to get to Shahar, so he sent out a message. He let him know that Shahar was still alive, that she needed saving. Everyone knows Salem doesn't care if the world burns. So King Tethra just had to sit back and let Salem find the cage for him."

"If the king had the Merrow here, why didn't he torture the answer out of him?"

She shrugged. "He didn't know the Merrow could help him. That was a deeply buried secret."

I took a shaking breath. "How long?" I asked, dread creeping up my throat. "How long would it take for the Fomorians to break free once the driftwood cage is gone?"

She shook her head. "No one knows exactly. A few weeks? I have no idea."

All this news was like a fist to my throat.

Shahar never deserved her fate. She'd never intended to

burn anything, and we'd simply used her for her magic. For all his talk of burning, that wasn't part of Salem's plan, either. It was just a consequence of his sister's freedom.

And yet—until something else was in place, the world needed her where she was. Or none of this would exist.

In any case, I wasn't about to waste any more time hashing out the details or the ethics. I had to get to Salem.

My magic crashed through my body. "Okay. They'll be heading for the sea. And once they plunge into the water, I can hunt them."

~

ONCE MORE, the river was carrying us in a rush of frothy, sparkling water. With the help of the gods, the river's direction had changed course entirely. Now, we were heading for the coast, for the wide sea.

As the river carried me, I was no longer sure if Lyria was with me. But it didn't matter. I didn't need her anymore. Here, in the water, I could already hear the Merrow's song again—still clear and distinct through the waves.

At last, the river opened up to the sea, not far from the dock where I'd arrived. I moved like a torpedo through the depths.

My magic propelled me through the sea, a storm of speed following after the sound of the music.

My heart was a wild beast. If Salem had taken the Merrow down from the sky, plunging into the water, that meant they'd found the right location. And it was almost too late...

I rushed forward, driven by desperation. Deeper and deeper into the water.

In the distance, I could see her—a beaming star in the

dark depths, like something from a dream. Her magic streamed around her in pearly rays of light. I rushed for her.

But when the Merrow's music went silent, panic slammed into me.

The Merrow was dead.

Salem had killed him, and he'd already found Shahar.

37

SALEM

J ust above the water, I released the ancient sorcerer's corpse—his head severed from his body by my hands. Maybe I couldn't kill Aenor for drowning Shahar, but it brought me great delight to rip the Merrow in two, after ripping the answers out of him.

I let my wings fade away and dove into the sea. The sorcerer's blood spilled through the water, staining it with black. But my eyes were on the driftwood cage, the water around it glowing bright. It was that perfect, silvery hue I recognized as my sister's.

The idea that my mate had done this to my sister was a cruel twist of fate I didn't want to contemplate any longer.

My anger was cold and clear as the light around the cage. What state would Shahar be in now, after all these years? Clearly, she was still alive, her magic beaming from her body, still radiating through the sea. But she must've lost her mind down here. No one could survive this hell with their senses intact.

By the time I reached her, I felt a sharp stabbing in my chest. I could hardly see her through the blazing starlight around her cage. Slowly, my eyes adjusted through the rays of unearthly beauty, and I saw a slumped, emaciated form in the cage. Like a living skeleton.

My heart stopped, and wrath flooded me. I wished I'd killed the Merrow slower. Gods, *Aenor* did this.

Now, to get Shahar out.

I pulled Lightbringer from her sheath, and holy fire flared along her blade.

A lock gleamed on the front of the driftwood cage. Golden magic glimmered around it. But Lightbringer could carve through anything.

Shahar's stolen power blazed over me, resplendent in the waves. It melded with my own until I almost felt like a god again.

Through the water, I could hear someone screaming my name, and I froze.

The sea dulled and muted the screaming, but I could still hear it. Aenor's voice.

I whirled in the water and caught a glimpse of her coming for me. That infernal sea glass gleamed in her hand, destined for my heart. When she'd said that it was only the wine, that she felt nothing for me, I'd felt some-thing crack in my chest. And here she was, coming for my life.

She'd actually do it, wouldn't she? If she had to, my own mate would carve my heart out rather than allow me to save Shahar. It felt as if she were sticking that shard into my heart now, carving it out.

I was a creature entirely unlovable—even when nature should compel my mate to love me. Shahar was the one who'd loved me, and only her.

I stared at Aenor. Would she return to Lyr when she'd finished with me? The thought of that made me want to turn the world into a blazing inferno. *Join my hell with me, all of you...*

And there she was—still managing to turn my thoughts away from my true task.

Only a few minutes left before Aenor would be upon me, jamming sea glass into my aorta. I turned back to my slumped sister.

I swung my sword through the water, lightning fast. The blade sliced cleanly through the lock, and the cage door creaked open. Instantly, Shahar's magic snapped back inside her frail body. Her back arched, arms flung back, face grimacing.

With my heart thundering, I yanked the door open the rest of the way.

My stomach turned at her state. She was obviously agonized. I reached into the cage to grab her around her protruding ribs. A thin layer of flesh covered her bones, nothing more. As gently as I could, I lifted her out of the cage, her body rigid as bone, gleaming with her magic.

I glanced through the water at Aenor.

She wasn't far from us now. I clutched Shahar tighter. Once I got to the surface, I'd be able to fly from here, to help my sister heal completely.

As I swam, I watched Shahar's eyes snap open. Under the water, she started to scream, sucking in water. Eyes wide with fear, arms flailing, she had the wild stare of a madwoman, no longer herself. Her silver hair, once lustrous, had become gnarled and untamed. It fell into her eyes in ragged hanks. I wrapped my arms around her, trying to calm her beneath the waves so she'd stop sucking in water. I kicked my legs, hurrying her to the surface.

In the distance, I caught a glimpse of Aenor again, her

blue hair bright in the murky water. Anger poisoned my heart at the sight of her.

But her attention wasn't on me. It was on the seafloor. I forced my attention away from her.

Shahar needed me more. Shahar was barely alive.

I held her tight, moving as fast as I could. When we reached the surface, my twin's shrieking deafened me.

But just as my mate had promised, I could feel the sea heating around me. Already it was getting hotter. It seemed her visions had been real.

38

AENOR

S alem pulled his sister from the sea, and the waters heated around me.

Hell was coming for us all.

Already, a molten red fissure was opening in the seafloor —so narrow you could hardly see it. But I could feel it. The heat pulsed through the water, turning my skin pink.

My magic slid through my body like nectar as I tried to cool the waters around me.

But as I started moving for the fissures, a burst of magic pounded through the sea, slamming into me with the force of a torpedo. Propelled by a hot stream of water, I rushed toward the surface, unable to stop it. It forced me upward, heating my skin.

The force of the blast sent me hurtling into the air, and I came down hard into the hot salt water. As my body hit the sea, I dropped the sea glass. I scrambled to get control again as the blast simmered down, and I conjured my cooling magic.

When I looked up in the air, I saw him—the fallen angel with his broken sister in his arms. He was so far away that I could hardly see him—just a hint of twilight bathing his wings.

The sight of him leaving felt like a blade between my ribs. I wondered if he realized he'd left me in a boiling sea. But why would I expect him to stay? He'd never pretended to be anything other than evil.

Men are wolves... Unlike most, at least he admitted it. And that was basically what he had going for him.

But I didn't have time to stew in this. My darling mate had created hell on earth—*again*—and I had to fix it. If I didn't, the world would begin turning to cinders, one tree at a time, one person at a time.

Treading water, I surveyed my surroundings. I was swimming near a grassy, rocky island. The sight of it brushed at the edges of my memory, and it occurred to me that it must have been where I'd helped the Merrow. I'd stood there a century ago, drunk in the night, and we'd sunk the driftwood cage that had brought Salem into my life.

Cold magic spilled from me, cooling the water around me. I peered under the surface again, trying to formulate a plan. Before I'd left Acre, Lyr had helped me memorize a spell—one that I could use to summon him if I needed him. And Lyr, with his World Key, could summon the other institutes, each with their own keys. We could have a small army here within minutes.

Except—Lyr might show up with a collar to bind my magic. And without my magic, we could lose the battle against the Fomorians.

I peered at the seafloor, sharpening my eyes to see through the murk. The explosion had forced the thin fissure open wider, and it now yawned as a red crack, nearly large enough for a person to fit through.

I conjured a burst of my magic, and it rose up my spine,

curling between my ribs. I filled my chest with the power of the sea and slid beneath the waves. Under the water, I exhaled breaths of streaming ice. Frozen currents spilled out around me, cooling the sea.

I swam just a little deeper, my eyes on the widening crack. Maybe I could stop this now, somehow.

Sea magic hummed along my limbs and spilled out from my body. The full force of my power shot through the ocean. The power electrified me, and I felt at one with the ancient sea. It was as if all sea life sighed in relief with my magic.

And yet—that fissure in the seafloor was still opening wider. And as it did, the heat began roiling up toward me again.

Shadows crawled over my heart at the sight of fingers gripping the edge of the fissure. Now, two hands were protruding from the molten red opening. The seafloor seemed to rumble.

I heard the sound of croaking voices whispering around me, a chorus of them.

We are... the oldest ones. We are... the buried ones. You made us... suffer. We will punish...

I felt as if poison spilled through my blood at the sound of them. They spoke in unison, their voices legion...

As the first Fomorian crawled through, I flung out my wrist to make a blade of ice. I could kill him, just like I'd killed the others.

With the wild power of my magic racing through my mind, my thoughts were going a million miles a minute. The glowing red crevasse burned like the sun, and the Fomorians' voices slithered over my skin.

As I readied myself for battle with the first Fomorian, I caught sight of another one, crawling from the widening chasm.

Then another, and another. Until half a dozen were crawling from the crevasse, heads sparking red in the gloom. They were fiery death embodied. My mind flickered with images of blackened fields and forests. Withered plants, cities of dust.

Fear slid over my heart like shadows across the moon.

I conjured the full force of my magic within my chest. Then I let it explode from me in a rush of power. I watched as the Fomorians' flames wavered, then snuffed out. My chest unclenched a little.

Quiet and cool again.

Except more of them were coming out now, the red crack widening in the ocean floor like a wicked smile. And within moments, the fire from their bodies was blazing again—rekindled.

We are... the oldest ones.... the buried ones...

The wild power of the sea roared in me, and I readied my sword to defend it.

When they rushed for me, heads blazing, I sparked into action. Speed and fury raced through me, and I cut through one after another, whirling with the speed of a sea god beneath the waves.

Their severed bodies drifted to the bottom of the sea. But that crack was opening wider, gleaming. The seafloor rumbled, and I could feel it coming. The whole godsdamn Fomorian army, about to burst forth, like demons from a womb.

Even with my power, I couldn't take on an entire army alone. They'd surround me, burn me, then move on to the rest of the world.

My stomach sank.

I needed warriors. An entire army of knights.

Godsdamn it. I had to summon Lyr. I had to trust he'd at least fight the battle correctly, even if we had our differences.

I turned to swim for the island. Rushing through the waves, I was heading for the shore with a speed that churned and frothed the waters around me.

The windswept, rocky island protruded from the water. I'd been here a lifetime ago, committing a crime buried by time and water.

I gasped in the heating air, trying to get my bearings as I rose from the sea. Barefoot, I stood on the warm rocks. Already, the seawater was evaporating from my skin, leaving a crusted layer of salt all over me. I sucked in a hot breath, my throat parched.

If we didn't stop them, they would blight every gods-damn tree and ignite every blade of grass.

I snatched a broken seashell from the shallow waves then cut it into my palm, wincing as I did. Blood dripped into the water, and I chanted the spell that Lyr had taught me.

They'd be here, soon. The Knights of Acre would call every knight from every court, every institute, to fight them.

At least, I freaking hoped so.

While I waited for Lyr and his knights to arrive, I waded back into the water, then dipped my head under the surface. I closed my eyes, my spirit melding with the ocean.

When I exhaled, it radiated out from my body in crystalline streams, cooling the water. With my rising desperation, this burst of magic felt more intense, streaming down to the crevasse. As I stepped out of the water, I saw shimmering ice rippling out from my body. Icy rain fell from the air, cooling the island, and frost formed on the rocks. A few chunks of ice floated in the waves.

"Aenor." Lyr's voice boomed behind me, and I whirled.

Right after that burst of ice magic was a hell of a time for him to arrive. It would look a lot like what he'd been afraid of this whole time.

And yet... he had no binding collar with him.

He stared at me, shadows darkening the air around him. A portal yawned open behind him, and the other knights began crawling from it.

"What are you doing?" His voice was cold as the rain.

My fingers twitched, my magic humming over my body. "They're here. The Fomorians. They're real. Salem set them free when he saved his sister, and they're going to burn the world down. I need your help to kill them. We need every knight you can summon."

I stared as Melisande crept from the portal, her orange wings returned to her body. "What the hells is going on?"

"They're real. The Fomorians," I said. "If you don't believe me, take a look at what's crawling out from under the waves. You need to summon all the knights. All of them from around the world."

Lyr narrowed his eyes at me. "You weren't able to kill Salem."

Gods, I didn't have time for disapproval. Anyway... "I wasn't. So we've covered that, and let's move on."

His gaze shot over my shoulder, eyes widening. I whirled to see three Fomorians rising from the waves, heads blazing with fire.

When I turned, I saw Lyr unsheathe his sword. He cursed under his breath, and I heard the other knights suck in their breaths.

At least we were all on the same page now.

I looked back at the Fomorians. Only three of them so far, and I could probably take them from here. Seawater gleamed over their gnarled bodies, but it quickly evaporated in the air. The sight of them sent cold shards of rage right through me, and I let my magic build in my chest. It rushed up my spine, and when I flung out my arms, blades of ice shot out from my fingertips. They pierced each one of the monsters in their hearts.

Gwydion took a step closer to me. "Bloody hell."

I held out my hand in the dry air. "Can you feel it? Can you feel the air heating around us?"

Lyr rushed forward, crashing into the waves, diving under for a moment. When he turned back to us, his eyes had gone black. "I see dozens of them crawling from the crack. Aenor is right. I think we'll be facing an army of them soon."

The other knights stood on the rocks, swords ready, eyes alert.

Lyr's gaze pierced me for a moment, then he rushed from the water, heading back to the portal. He stood over it, his body gleaming with gold, hair whipping around his head as he chanted above it.

That was just like him, wasn't it? Just starting to do something without explaining what he was doing. But once I heard him chanting a spell and saw the World Key glowing at his neck, I understood he was summoning the other knights.

Hot waves lapped at my feet.

When the next wave of Fomorians emerged from the water, we were ready. We crossed into the heating waters to fight them, their bodies burning as we met them. The setting sun washed us all in crimson light, and blood spilled in the water. I moved in a whirlwind of cold speed, my sword cutting through hot flesh. As I killed them, a hissing sound rose around us, like drops of water on hot rocks.

But even as we fought them, the Fomorians were

speaking to us as they rose from the sea. "We are the ancient ones," they croaked. "The forgotten ones... We are the buried. We will punish you..." And then the words that sent a stab of guilt shooting through my chest: "Salem set us free."

Salem. The word now was a blade of ice in my heart.

A glance behind me showed me that Lyr was already bringing more knights into the fray, armor gleaming in the hot sun. And around them, the trees and grass were withering, blackening. Already, the island's grass had browned. Nausea rose in my gut. This had only just begun, and already the life was wilting around us.

Screams curdled my blood, and I whirled, blade ready. Fomorians were starting to burn some of the knights. My mouth went dry, and I drove my icy sword into another attacker.

Salem set us free...

I could have stopped this. My damn soulmate was the one to unleash it.

We are the forgotten ones...

From the corner of my eye, I winced at the sight of Melisande, her wings blazing with flames. She was trying to run into the water to douse them, but another Fomorian gripped her by the hair. Burning Fomorians surrounded her, and she screamed.

Around us, the knights and the ancient fire fae were clashing, bodies burning. The air smelled of seared flesh.

This was a scene from hell.

From Salem's cave.

I moved farther into the hot salt water, determination sliding through me.

We wouldn't win this with swords, would we?

I had to go down there, into the hot water. I had to go

down to the mouth of the beast and use all my magic to seal it up with ice.

Fighting off the burning Fomorians around me, I rushed deeper into the hot sea.

Then I dove.

The water felt scalding against my body, but I used my magic to try to cool myself down.

Did Salem feel bad, I wondered? Or did he have what he wanted, and he'd moved on? A tumble in the grass with his mate, then he'd moved on to his real destiny.

Icy anger buzzed through my body. I dodged between the Fomorians in the water, heading for the hot crevasse.

My heart had shattered into pieces, and anger spilled through my body like dark ink. At least wrath gave me clarity.

A broken heart left you so cold.

I could use the cold right now.

The chasm was a wide, gaping wound now, like a slash in a pregnant belly. And the Fomorians spilled out of it. Molten heat was ripping open the ocean floor. I fought through the blistering water, heading right for the crevasse. As I swam, I let my magic build in my body, stronger and stronger, until I felt powerful as the divine combustion of a star.

At the bottom, where fire had ripped the seafloor open, I gripped the hot rocks. I felt my fingers burning.

Salem left me here.

I couldn't even remember if that thought was rational anymore. I only knew that it broke me open and hollowed me out, like an empty oyster shell.

The sea glass glittered on the rocks beneath me, and I swam for it. Snatching it up, I carved it deep into my arm. One more sacrifice to the god of the sea...

My blood spilled through the water.

"God of the rivers and sea, grant me the strength to seal the crack. Grant me the strength to stop the Fomorians."

In the hollows of my mind, the sea god spoke in a whisper: *I'll need more than blood...* The dark waters sucked up the blood greedily, a vortex whirling around me, hungry for more sacrifice.

Alarm bells rang in my mind, but that seemed like a problem for another time.

I gathered all my cold rage and let it build in my chest to a wild pitch, an explosive force of power.

Then, when I felt my body was about to burst at the seams with magic, I flung back my arms. I unleashed the full force of it. The icy power of the sea exploded out of me, rumbling over the ocean floor in an atomic blast of cold. The vibrations trembled through the rocks, through my bones.

Ice spread out from my body, freezing the Fomorians in place. Their limbs contorted, fingers bent. The flames on their heads snuffed out in the dark water, eyes bulging with horror. Then, one by one, their bodies fractured into tiny pieces of ice.

I loosed a breath, then looked down at the seafloor below me. The fissure filled with gleaming ice. It spread out, sealing the Fomorians in. As it covered the red glow, cold shadows swallowed up the world around me.

In the dark and the cold, I floated.

Above me, the battle raged, but there were no more Fomorians getting out. The knights had to kill only those who'd escaped.

Darkness pooled around me, and I felt a bone-deep chill. I couldn't leave here, could I? I'd be here for good, keeping the crevasse shut. Through the water, I felt the battle growing quieter. I thought the knights were regaining control now.

My hair wafted around me, and the sea grew quiet. Above me, the sunlight grew dimmer. Salem had left me, and I felt like I was falling through the darkness. It was like someone had distilled the essence of a million lonely Sunday evenings, drowned me with it.

I looked up at the surface of the sea, flickering red with the flames of the Fomorians. It looked like the flames were dying out now, the knights winning the battle.

Thorns twisted around the inside of my chest. This was what I'd done to Shahar, wasn't it?

All those years ago, Mama had gotten me drunk when it was time to drown Shahar. But she always had a clear head. She always knew exactly what she was doing.

What was so off about me that I couldn't be trusted? She used to say that I could wither plants with the looks I gave when a temper struck me, and I could poison the mood in a room. I made people nervous.

I never knew if I was supposed to be strong like Mama, or sweet like the lithe, smiling river fae. The pleasant ones who laughed and danced and sang at court.

I just had this gnawing feeling, deep in the hollows of my mind, that I'd never been quite right.

Above the crevasse, I traced my fingertips over the large swath of ice.

With a shock of surprise, I realized I'd felt right with Salem. Maybe because he was more twisted than I was—no judgment from him. And even as he made my heart race, he made my thoughts quiet. At times, he drew my attention so sharply that the chaos calmed. He'd taught me how to channel my magic so it didn't overwhelm me.

At least, until I'd come at him with the sea glass, and he'd left in the boiling sea.

I stared at the world of ice beneath me.

Wasn't I enough now? I'd closed the chasm with ice. I'd stopped the attack. I'd fixed it.

So maybe I wasn't quite right, and maybe I made people nervous, but I got the job done in the end.

I just had to stay here, forever, and everything could be fine.

I looked through the murky water at the empty drift-wood cage, its door hanging open like a gaping jaw. As the sound of the Fomorians faded, the only noise was the creaking of the door.

I'd finally gotten the silence I craved. I'd gotten the job done.

But webs of frost spread over my heart.

39

SALEM

My wings lifted me into the air above the sea. Gripping Shahar tightly to me, I glanced down at the sea. Shahar was still flailing, shrieking.

But all I could think was—maybe I didn't care if the world burned. But I cared if Aenor did.

This was supposed to be my moment of victory. I'd saved Shahar, and I was on my way to achieving my destiny. We'd become gods again.

As I left Aenor behind, a jagged ache hollowed out my chest. Whatever came next, I had to believe Aenor would survive. I'd given her the immense sea power back—protection against whatever she faced.

Maybe Lyr didn't have faith in her powers, but I did.

And yet, as my wings carried us into the air, fear spilled through my blood.

I laid my sister down on an island's grassy shore. She'd gone limp again, eyes closed. Our gleaming magic twined together, shimmering with silver on the mist.

I should feel whole again, reunited with my twin.

This was my great moment of victory. The first part of my destiny achieved.

This was a moment of jubilation. Red light crawled over the sky, soaking my skin in ruddy rays. The goddess Anat—my mother—heralded my triumph.

Next, we'd ascend to the heavens, Shahar and I. Just as I'd wanted for eons, I'd be leaving this earth for good—this place of torment.

People thought Gehenna was hell. My little fire pit. And, of course, it was. But the truth was that all of this was hell. Here, on the ground, cruelty reigned.

I brushed my sister's silver hair out of her face. "Shahar."

Her eyes looked dull as worn rocks.

A flicker of panic sparked in my mind. Was her mind gone for good?

I cupped her face, and her eyes sharpened—pale blue streaked with coral. Those colors had lived in my mind since the dawn of time.

Her silver hair floated around her head like she was still underwater. At last, she focused on me.

My chest unclenched a little. She was here, with me, my twin. She slid one of her hands over mine, staring into my eyes. "Salem." Her voice cracked.

"It took me a long time to find you. I didn't know you were still alive."

Her eyes flicked to the sky, and she stared at the setting sun. That was where we belonged. Away from here.

I only had a few days left—a deadline etched in stone. Would Anat help us rise to the heavens now, or did I still have some task I needed to complete?

"Salem," she said again, her gaze locked on me, now sharp and keen as the morning star. "What's wrong with you?"

What was wrong with *me*? I'd just dredged her up from the bottom of the ocean, screaming and flailing. I'd saved her. I was fine. "What are you talking about? Everything is going according to plan. We're going to return to the heavens."

"So what's wrong with you?" she repeated. "Why do you look like you want to jump off a cliff?"

My sister and I were never ones for small talk. But I would have preferred it right now—a bit of "what have you been doing in the past one hundred years," or "let me catch you up on my century in the watery sea hell," or "how about this sun we're getting?" Instead, she was reading my soul and forcing me to confront it. A habit of hers. And already, my mind was on Aenor. The water lapping at the shore now felt hot, steam curling off it.

What if I'd left my mate to die?

It wasn't really a thrilling moment of triumph when you felt like your ribs were piercing your heart.

This wasn't a victory. This was bones scattered over a battlefield, crushed into the dirt. This was falling from the heavens, my soul ripped from my body.

All wrong.

"I have to go, Shahar." I pulled away from her. "I'll find you again."

Shahar's silver-blue magic beamed around her body now. "Fix whatever it is. I'm going to find my cats." She spoke to me in the language of the gods, and her voice reverberated in my mind. Hardly a whisper.

Did she realize that all of her cats had died over a hundred years ago? I'd have to catch her up on that later when the sea wasn't boiling my soulmate alive.

My wings lifted me into the evening sky, and my body cast a shadow over the water as I flew. The sea wind whipped over my body. I flew back to where I had left Aenor, my heart pounding against my ribs like a war drum.

My destiny was in the heavens, the celestial realm. But before I left—I needed Aenor to be safe.

My soul commanded it.

When I swept over the island where I'd left her, I found a battle raging. Smoke curled into the air, some of the knights burning with flames. Lyr was among them, moving in a maelstrom of dark magic. But the knights seemed to be winning the battle.

One of them threw something at me—a spear. *Idiot.*

I arced out of the way. The scent of burned flesh curled into the air. A red banner of fear unfurled in me. It smelled like Gehenna.

Now, my blood roared in my ears. Frantically, I searched the battle for signs of Aenor, for her blue hair gleaming among all the rabble. I didn't see her among them, and dread swept over me like dark smoke.

Had I left her to die?

Over my thundering pulse, I tried to think clearly. I would have felt it. If she'd died, I would have felt the last ember of light go out in my chest. I was sure of it.

In my panic, I'd nearly forgotten the enchantment. I could find her, of course, wherever she went. Fear made people stupid, didn't it? What a useless emotion.

Swooping through the air, I let my magic boom around me. She'd hear it, wherever she was. She'd know I was coming for her.

In my mind's eye, I saw her then, trapped beneath the icy water—a tomb of cold. I felt her loneliness carving through me. Then the sharp tug of my bond to her. It was like a cord pulled me to her through the air.

I angled my wings, diving fast for the water. Just before I

hit the surface, I let my wings fade away. The velocity of my flight propelled me fast through the cool water.

Her magic skimmed over my skin. She was chilling the waters even now.

It took me a few moments before I saw her beautiful glow, the pearly green and blue that lured me closer. My siren, drawing me in. At the seafloor, she floated by herself just above a large swath of ice.

Her body pulled me closer like the moon pulled the tide.

Her eyes were on me. Not angry, just curious. Her magic beamed around her.

As I reached her, her brow furrowed. "I can't leave here."

Her morgen's voice carried through the water. I had no such skill. I mouthed, "Why?"

"I have to seal the opening to the Fomorian world." A few bubbles escaped her mouth.

A voice knelled around us, the somber, alien tone of a god. *More than blood...*

I glanced down at Aenor's bleeding arm. She'd made a sacrifice, but it wasn't enough. That was the thing with gods. It was never enough.

As I looked down at the swath of ice again, it seemed to be melting.

"Salem!" she shouted. "You can't distract me. Can you go now, please? I can barely keep this magic going when I'm focusing."

I watched her as she concentrated again, conjuring her magic. A burst of power beamed out from her body, slamming into my chest. My body absorbed it.

But I could feel it—the rumbling, the trembling of the ocean floor. Aenor's magic was considerable, but it wasn't a god's magic. They'd needed someone with Shahar's power to stop the Fomorians from ripping the ocean floor wide open.

Where could I take her, away from this place, where she'd be safe? Let the rest of the world burn. Aenor could live in a rocky cave in the arctic.

I watched her working her magic while I fantasized about things that made no sense. What sort of life would that be—alone in a cave, walls heating around her? Worse than death.

The roaring beneath the earth grew louder, reverberating over my taut muscles.

Beneath us, the hot ravine in the ocean's floor was cracking open once more. Dread slid through my veins like venom. Before me, I could already see my destiny turning to ash…

A blast of heat exploded from the fissure, searing the water around us. I couldn't burn, but she could.

Aenor's scream pierced the water, and I watched her skin turning red, then blistering. Panic hit me like a bolt of lightning, driving all rational thought from my mind. It was like I was the one burning.

She'd die here, literally boil to death before me if I didn't stop this. When the blast of heat died down, I grabbed her face in my hands.

Her eyes gleamed with pain, skin ravaged.

"Fix this," I mouthed.

It was the same thing Shahar had said to me, minus any mention of cats.

Aenor wasn't meeting my eyes, too lost in the pain. I turned to swim away from her.

The door of the driftwood cage swung in and out in the hot water, like an arm beckoning me close.

I didn't give a fuck about the rest of the world, but I cared about Aenor like she was a part of me.

I swam into the driftwood cage—my prison—and closed the door. The lock sealed itself, gleaming with magic.

As I felt the cage's magic rip all my power from my body, I had only one thought in my mind: *Aenor is strong, and she will fix this.*

40

AENOR

I stared into the driftwood cage. Salem's body slumped against the side, and his pearly magic beamed around it. I looked down at my skin, burned from the hot blast of water. As his magic streamed over it, my skin began to heal. Although his magic was warm, it felt like a soothing balm on my skin.

From above, I could still hear a few croaking whispers drifting through the waves... *We are the buried ones...*

The driftwood cage was again closed, the lock gleaming with gold magic.

The shock of what he'd done had robbed me of all rational thought.

"Salem," I said.

He lay there, his eyes closed, his dark lashes stark against his skin. His muscles still looked tense, but his eyes were closed. Was he in pain as his magic was pulled from his body?

I wrapped my fingers around the bars. It felt wrong—his body always radiated heat, but all the warmth was outside the cage now. When I reached for him through the bars, brushing my fingertips over his leg, he felt cold.

My heart twisted. *This* would not do.

Was it to save the world—or just to save me? Either way, I wanted him out of there.

I'd been so intent on Salem that I nearly forgot to look at the crevasse beneath me, or the threat of the Fomorians.

When I looked down at the seafloor, I found the crevasse sealing again.

I stared at Salem, my mind roiling.

So *this* was my mate. A man who delighted in telling everyone how evil he was, then sacrificed himself at the bottom of the sea.

He'd been talking about his destiny since I'd met him. And I still didn't know what he'd had in mind, but surely he wasn't meant for this. This was a living death.

Above, the sounds of battle faded completely, and the whispers of the Fomorians faded above us.

I stayed there with him for what seemed like ages, studying his face.

Fix this, he'd said.

I didn't know how, but I wouldn't get the answers down here.

I turned, swimming for the surface. So quiet now. I could hardly hear the music of any creature.

On the rocky island shore, Lyr stood by himself, silvered in the moonlight. Dark blood streaked his armor, and bodies lay strewn around him like broken toys.

His powerful body glowed with gold, and his pale eyes pierced the darkness. "How did you do it? You stopped the world from ripping open."

I slumped down on the rocks, my body exhausted. "I stopped them for a little while. Then Salem did the rest.

Right now, he's locked himself in the Merrow's cage at the bottom of the sea."

Shadows leaked around Lyr's body, staining the gold magic with darkness. "Why would he do that? What does he get out of it?"

I rubbed my forehead. How did I explain this to Lyr? I didn't want to tell him Salem was my mate, or that I planned to get him out. None of this fit with Beira's vision, which meant Lyr would discard it. I supposed things had happened as she'd said—the Fomorians hadn't boiled the sea, my magic had spread ice out over the horizon.

It just wasn't quite as Lyr had imagined.

I let out a long sigh. "Why did he do it? I don't know." That, really, was the truth. "But he did, and the Fomorians are now trapped again. It's all over, Lyr. We can get on with our lives."

Lyr nodded, but his eyes had taken on a haunted expression, like he'd just drifted into the afterworld again.

I felt the air thin around us, and his wary eyes slid to me.

I had that feeling again—the one of not being quite right. I *scared* him.

"It's all over," I said again.

But it wasn't. Not with Salem entombed in the sea.

"I'm returning to Acre," Lyr said. "Gina is safe, returned to her hotel. She'd been living in a friend's hovel."

The distance between us was wide as an ocean, our conversation stiff.

And yet—he'd taken care of the person I cared about. "Thank you."

"Will you return to London?" he asked.

I had no idea what I was doing, only that I felt tethered to Salem right now. "I need to figure that out, Lyr. For now,

I'm just going to sit here among the carnage, breathing in the scent of death."

He gazed out over the sea. "I may have been wrong about the collar. Beira's predictions are not always direct. I saw the ice spread out over the landscape when I first arrived here, and I feared the worst. But I understand now." He looked at me again. "If you can control your power, you can keep it."

I narrowed my eyes at him. *Like it's your decision.*

He nodded, then turned away from me, the key glowing at his neck. I watched him chant the words for opening the portal, his body glowing. When he jumped through, and the portal sealed up once more, it was just me and the sound of the cold, lapping sea.

I crossed back into the cool waters, breathing in the scent of brine. Then I dove under the waves. Even from here by the shore, I could see the faint shimmer of Salem's light under the waves. It was brighter than Shahar's.

I hoped he was sleeping there, not conscious under a mask of sleep. Trapped.

If he could speak to me, he'd tell me to find Shahar, then get him out. And I would.

When I stepped out of the water again, I heard the rhythmic sound of oars splashing in the sea. On the gore-strewn rocks, I watched as a boat moved closer. The rower was lithe, with three birds flitting around his head.

Ossian?

As he drew closer, I saw his blond curls, threaded with flowers. A cloud of smoke bloomed around him.

I waded into the water to greet him, and the spray from the ocean washed over me.

He breathed out a cloud of smoke. "I felt shit going down through the waves. I felt Salem's magic through the water." His gaze slid over my shoulder to the carnage on the rocky island. "That your doing, was it?"

"Not entirely." I heaved a sigh, then crawled into Ossian's boat, and it rocked under me. "Salem took his sister's place under the water, and I need to find a way to fix this."

Ossian's eyes narrowed. "You've got to be joking. Why would he do that?"

"To stop the world from burning."

He leaned forward. "Since when has he cared about the world burning?"

Since he saw my skin blistering, I think. I shook my head. "Let's not worry about his motives."

"I'd say love would do that to a person, except I happen to know that Salem can't love. It's literally impossible."

An empty feeling rose in me. "Whatever his motives, I need to figure this out, as fast as I can. I know he's the devil and all that, but I want to get him out of his prison."

"And why would that be, Aenor?"

I cleared my throat. "Just seems like the right thing to do."

He started rowing, the water splashing over us. "Yeah. Better sort it out within days, ideally, or he misses his whole destiny thing. He'd get in a right mood about it. Start burning things again."

I blinked. "What is his destiny, exactly? It wasn't freeing his sister?"

Ossian leaned back in his boat as he rowed. "Oh, he didn't tell you? I thought you two must've bonded, what with you being alive and all. And him in a cage."

"We didn't get around to the destiny discussion. We were busy thinking about killing each other." And thinking about doing other things with each other, I supposed. "Where are we going, Ossian?"

"I have a house nearby. And I sense heartbreak."

I nodded. "Oh, here we go again."

"I owe you vodka and ice cream."

I stared at the dull gleam of light beneath the sea, my heart twisting. "Well, that actually sounds very appealing. And very necessary right now."

∽

IF YOU WANT to read more about Aenor now, she appears in the Shadow Fae series, in book four. This is a linked series.

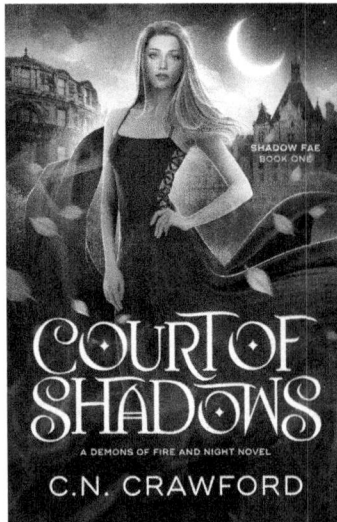

ACKNOWLEDGMENTS

Thanks to my supportive family, and to Michael Omer for his patient critiques and help managing my occasional panic. Thanks to Nick for his feedback and enthusiasm.

Robin and Arran are my fabulous editors for this book.

Thanks to my advanced reader team for their help, and to C.N. Crawford's Coven on Facebook!

ALSO BY C.N. CRAWFORD

For a full list of our books, check out our website.

https://www.cncrawford.com/books/

And a possible reading order.

https://www.cncrawford.com/faq/

Printed in Great Britain
by Amazon